A Valentine's gift for readers of
Harlequin American Romance.

Two heartwarming Valentine novellas from
two of your favorite authors.

Be Mine, Cowboy by Jane Porter ₦4
Hill Country Cupid by Tanya Michaels

ABOUT THE AUTHOR

Jane Porter is a small-town girl at heart. Growing up, she spent her vacations on her grandfather's cattle ranch in California, loving the golden foothills, oak trees and miles of farmland. When not playing cowgirl or camping with her family, she'd curl up with a book and get lost in her imagination. In her mind, she was never the geeky bookworm with the thick Coke-bottle glasses, but a princess, a magical fairy, a Joan-of-Arc crusader.

Her parents fed her imagination by taking the family to Europe for a year when Jane was thirteen. She loved everything about Europe, but was especially passionate about Italy and those gorgeous Italian men, which later inspired her first Harlequin Presents title, *The Italian Groom,* a story that married her love of farmland and ranches and sexy Italian heroes!

Since that first sale to Harlequin Presents in 2000, Jane has written over 30 books and novellas for Harlequin and she still gets excited about each new story.

Jane is always delighted to hear from her readers. You can email her at jane@janeporter.com, or write to Jane Porter, P.O. Box 789, San Clemente, CA 92674.

Three-time RITA® Award nominee **Tanya Michaels** writes about what she knows—community, family and lasting love! Her books, praised for their poignancy and humor, have received honors such as a Booksellers' Best Bet Award, a Maggie Award of Excellence and multiple readers' choice awards. She was also a 2010 *RT Book Reviews* nominee for Career Achievement in Category Romance. Tanya is an active member of Romance Writers of America and a frequent public speaker, presenting workshops to educate and encourage aspiring writers. She lives outside Atlanta with her very supportive husband, two highly imaginative children and a household of quirky pets, including a cat who thinks she's a dog and a bichon frise who thinks she's the center of the universe.

My Cowboy Valentine

JANE PORTER

TANYA MICHAELS

HARLEQUIN® AMERICAN ROMANCE®

ISBN-13: 978-0-373-75442-7

Recycling programs for this product may not exist in your area.

MY COWBOY VALENTINE
Copyright © 2013 Harlequin Books S.A.

The publisher acknowledges the copyright holder of the individual works as follows:

BE MINE, COWBOY
Copyright © 2013 by Jane Porter

HILL COUNTRY CUPID
Copyright © 2013 by Tanya Michna

HARLEQUIN®

www.Harlequin.com

Printed in U.S.A.

CONTENTS

Be Mine, Cowboy
JANE PORTER

Dear Reader,

I'm a hopeless romantic! I believe in love at first sight and true love, and am crazy about reunion romances—stories where a couple is torn apart by fate, but then later brought back together again, because this couple, of course, is destined to be together.

When the editors of Harlequin American Romance asked me to write a novella for this special Valentine's anthology with the wonderful Tanya Michaels, I jumped at the chance. With a Texan grandfather, I'm a huge fan of cowboy romances and used to write them before I started writing for Harlequin Presents. And while I love writing for Harlequin Presents, I don't get to do enough ranch stories, small-town settings and cowboy heroes, so this novella is very special to me.

In *Be Mine, Cowboy* you'll meet two of my favorite characters I've ever written—All-Around Cowboy champion Cade King and his first love, Rachel James. They met in Mineral Wells, Texas, when Rachel was just nineteen, and they fell head over heels in love. Their love was supposed to be a forever love, but Cade is a complex man with problems Rachel couldn't fix, and he walked away from her when she insisted he get help. But five years later, he shows up on her doorstep, and this time, Cade's not going anywhere. Like a true, tough, loyal cowboy, he's going to win his woman back and prove to her he isn't just a great cowboy, but he's become a great man.

I hope you'll enjoy *Be Mine, Cowboy*. I'm so proud to be part of this anthology with the talented Tanya Michaels!

Happy Valentine's Day!

Jane

For my son, Jake. A hero in the making.

Chapter One

It'd been a mild winter so far in Palo Pinto County, Texas, and this February afternoon the sun was once again shining, and the sky over the small ranch house was a cloudless swathe of pale blue.

The weatherman had said the unseasonably mild temperatures and dry conditions were supposed to hold through the weekend, which was a good thing as Rachel James's childhood friend Mia Jenkins was getting married tomorrow, and while the party tent might be heated and fully protected from the elements, no one liked slogging through muddy or slushy gardens in formal wear. Not the bride or the guests or the cake baker.

And Rachel was both a guest and the cake baker.

"What do you think?" Rachel asked as Mia swirled a finger across the frosting-covered spatula before popping her finger in her mouth.

Mia sighed, rolling her eyes with pleasure. "Yum. Heavenly. Melt-in-your-mouth buttercream with just the right amount of vanilla. How come my frosting never tastes this good?"

"Because you probably worry about the amount of sugar and butter in your icing. I don't." Rachel crossed her arms over her chest, creasing her white apron, feeling ridiculously pleased with herself as she studied the tiered wedding cake, all four layers swagged with delicate swells and scallops of icing that resembled Belgium lace. "You like the cake?"

"I *love* my cake. It's beyond gorgeous, and you know it, so stop fishing for compliments."

Rachel grinned and gathered the stainless-steel bowls, carrying them to the kitchen sink. As she turned the faucet on, her gaze lifted to the window and the view beyond. The kitchen window overlooked the small, fenced backyard, which seemed even smaller right now with the mountain of cardboard boxes stacked next to the detached garage. Her smile faded as she looked at the boxes. She'd been packing for weeks, was nearly done. Just had bedrooms and the kitchen stuff left to pack, and now that Mia's wedding cake was finished, Rachel could box up all of her baking things.

"Can't believe you're moving," Mia said, joining her at the sink and getting a glimpse of the U-Haul moving boxes outside.

Rachel made a soft, inarticulate sound as she turned the tap off. "Can't believe I lost Grandma's house. She'd die if she knew."

"Maybe it's a good thing she's already dead, then," Mia said drily.

"That's horrible!" Rachel spluttered, reaching for a dish towel, uncertain if she should laugh or cry or both.

"It is, but it's the truth."

For a moment Rachel struggled to speak and then she blurted, "Today would have been her birthday. I've been thinking about her all day."

"Oh, Rachel! I know you still miss her so much."

"I do. I really do."

Mia wrapped an arm around Rachel's shoulder and gave it a squeeze. "But knowing your grandmother, she would have been beside herself if she realized what she did to you, deferring her property taxes all those years."

For a moment Rachel let herself relax into the hug. It

was so rare that she revealed weakness, so rare that she took comfort from anyone, but she needed the hug right now. It was brutal losing her home, but she wasn't the only one this had happened to, and she wasn't going to cry over spilled milk. What happened had happened, and there was nothing she could do about it but move forward and have a good attitude.

Gently, Rachel disengaged from the hug. "It's not Grandma's fault. I knew money was tight and yet I let her help us… she was always giving to us, trying to help me with bills. I should have asked her where the money was coming from."

"She probably wouldn't have told you, though. She loved Tommy so much. Loved having the two of you with her."

Mia was right about that, Rachel thought. Grandma loved having family around. She always said family gave life meaning.

Mia looked anxious. "You're really okay moving while we're gone?"

"Have a moving company and everything. I'm good. And you shouldn't be worrying about us. You're getting married tomorrow. This is about you right now."

"But I hate your new apartment complex. It's awful—"

"It's fine. And it's cheap, as well as close to Tommy's sitter."

"I wish I'd had the money to help you."

"Mia, stop."

Mia nibbled on her thumb. "I can name a half-dozen folks right now who would have helped you if you'd asked—"

"Not going to impose on people. This is my problem. Not theirs."

"But they're your friends—"

"And I appreciate them, but I'm not going to ask for handouts."

"It'd be a loan, Rachel."

"A loan I can't pay back." Rachel shot her a dark look.

"Cakes pay basic bills, but they won't make me rich." Peeling off her apron, she glanced at the clock on the old kitchen stove. "Isn't your rehearsal starting at four?"

Mia checked her watch and shrieked. "It's almost four already, and I haven't picked up the bridesmaids' dresses or the shoes, and I still have a twenty-five minute drive—"

"Don't panic," Rachel answered, rushing with her to the front door, "and don't drive crazy. You'll get there, and you're the bride. No one's going anywhere," she added, swinging open the front door.

"You're the best, Rache." Mia took a step and then froze on the doorstep. "Cade?" Mia squeaked, eyes widening with surprise.

Rachel glanced past Mia to the tall cowboy on the porch, and the air caught in her throat.

Cade.

Cade.

Her heart stuttered, staggered, and she blinked, certain he'd disappear, certain he was an apparition. But even after blinking twice, he was still there, one hand hooked on his massive silver belt buckle, and a bouquet of yellow roses in the other, six-two without his boots and cowboy hat, and even taller wearing both. He was wearing both.

"Hello, darlin'," he said. "Mia," he added, giving Rachel's friend a nod.

Mia blushed. "Long time no see."

"It's been a while," he agreed, his tone grave.

Rachel could only stare at him as she dragged air into her lungs, hating the bittersweet pain that filled her heart. It'd been five years since Cade King had walked away from her, and he'd gone without a backward glance, shattering her heart into a thousand pieces.

"Congratulations on your third consecutive title. We're all proud of you—" Mia broke off as she caught sight of Rachel's expression. "Anyway, I was just leaving. Take care."

"You, too, Mia."

And then with a swift, speculative glance in Rachel's direction, Mia was gone, dashing down the front steps, heading for the driveway.

For a moment the only sound was Mia's car door slamming and her engine starting. Rachel swallowed hard and forced herself to look at Cade, still unable to believe he was here. But he was here. And he was even bigger and more ruggedly handsome than she'd remembered.

"Cade," she whispered, shocked, numb, dumbfounded. He had been completely absent from her life for over five years...so why was he here now?

"Rachel."

"What...what....are you doing here?"

"It's your grandmother's birthday. Brought her some flowers."

He'd remembered Grandma. She ground her teeth together, her eyes burning. Was this real? Was *he* real? And God forgive her, was he sober?

"I probably should have called," he added gruffly, "but I wanted to surprise her."

Rachel blinked and struggled to find her voice. Just when she'd thought everyone had forgotten her grandmother, Cade showed up with birthday flowers. Yellow roses. Her favorite. "That's nice of you."

Dusky color warmed his high, hard cheekbones. "Can I come in?"

She nodded, stepping back to open the door wider. He dipped his head and, crossing her threshold, he removed his cowboy hat, revealing his glossy black hair. "Is this a bad time?"

It had been years since she had last seen him. Years since she had last heard his warm honeyed accent, a voice so rich with the Texas south that even in winter she felt the heat of an invisible sun and the caress of a breeze. He looked surprisingly good…but different, too. He was leaner than she remembered, tanner, healthier, his blue eyes so clear.

"No," she said unsteadily, aware that she'd need to pick up Tommy by four forty-five but she had a half hour. She closed the front door behind Cade, catching a whiff of his fragrance as she stepped towards him. The scent was light and a little spicy, but it suited him, and made her head spin.

"Mia looks well," he said.

"She's doing great."

His gaze searched hers for a moment. "And you? How are you?"

This was strange…so strange, she thought. "Good. I'm good."

"Glad to hear it."

For a moment neither of them seemed to know what to say and Rachel's stomach did a series of somersaults that made her wish she'd eaten something today to counter the cups of coffee she'd drunk earlier. Then she remembered her manners. "Would you like to sit down?" she asked, and subtly tugged on the hem of her red T-shirt, drawing it lower over the waistband of her faded jeans, glad she'd gotten rid of the shapeless apron. She wished she could pull the rubber band out of her hair, but that would be too obvious.

"Yes. Thank you."

She led the way into the small, oddly formal living room, with its old-fashioned Empire sofa and matching armchairs, all still upholstered in its original yellow silk. Cade sat down on the edge of the sofa cushion, looking far too big for the antique sofa's dainty lines.

"Would you like something to drink—" She flushed. "Coffee, tea," she added hurriedly.

"I'm fine. Thank you."

She slowly took a chair opposite him, hands folding in her lap to hide the fact they were shaking. She was trembling. None of this seemed real, especially when he was looking at her so intently, his blue eyes fringed by those long black lashes, startlingly clear, his gaze piercing, unnervingly direct.

"I had some business in Mineral Wells today," he said, "and since I got to town early, I thought I'd stop by and wish Sally happy birthday and see how you two were doing." He glanced around the bare living room. "Is Sally even here?"

"No."

The corners of his mouth curved. "Is she out with the girls or having her hair done?"

Rachel felt sick. She wanted to throw up. This was awful. Everything about this was awful. "Cade, Grandma died two and a half years ago."

"What?"

She nodded miserably. "Cancer."

He sat back heavily and set the flowers aside, placing them on the cushion next to him. "Cancer? When…how?"

She laced and unlaced her fingers, her eyes gritty, her throat aching with suppressed emotion. "Lung cancer—"

"She didn't smoke."

"I guess you don't need to smoke to get it." Rachel blinked hard, struggled to smile, but failed. "We thought she had a cold that just wouldn't go away. Bronchitis. By the time she finally went to see a doctor, there was nothing anyone could do. We found out early June it was cancer, and by July 5 she was gone."

"Aw, shit." Cade's deep, rough voice broke. His head dropped, and he covered his eyes with one hand.

For several minutes neither said anything, and the room was silent. Rachel squeezed her hands together and fought to hold back her tears. Cade's reaction made her teary and emotional, and yet it almost felt good to feel so much…it was almost a relief to know someone else had loved her grandmother, too.

"I'm sorry, Rache," he said, his voice raspy and raw. He lifted his head and looked at her, his dense lashes damp, the blue of his eyes almost aquamarine with sorrow. "You know, I promised her I'd always stay in touch with her. Promised her that I'd always be family—" He shook his head, once, twice. "Was she…did she…suffer a lot…in the end?"

"They tried to make her as comfortable as they could."

His head dropped again and he ran a hand over his eyes. "Wish I'd been here. Wish I could have been here for both of you."

Rachel couldn't even respond to that. Her heart felt as though it was breaking all over again. She dragged in a breath of air, then exhaled, struggling to keep it together. "It happened a long time ago, Cade," she murmured. "And Grandma didn't hold grudges. She believed people were a work in progress, and she'd be thrilled you won the All-Around title two more times after she was gone. She followed your career. Was probably your biggest fan."

His eyes watered and a small muscle popped in his jaw near his ears. "Even though I'd broken your heart?"

Rachel looked away, bit into her lip. This was so brutal, and so unexpected. She wasn't sure she could take much more of this. But Grandma had taught her to be strong, and she would be strong now…even if it killed her. "Grandma always said you'd find your feet again. She said you were one of those fallen angels just waiting to regrow your wings."

"I wish that were true," Cade said regretfully. "But I haven't grown wings yet."

"Maybe they'll still come."

"If you believe in miracles," he answered drily, his firm mouth twisting, the corners of his eyes creasing.

His crooked smile made her breath catch and her pulse quicken. For a moment he looked—and sounded—so much like the sexy, laid-back, self-deprecating cowboy she'd loved so long ago that the years seemed to fall away and she gulped another breath of air, overwhelmed. Dazzled.

"I used to," she said, smiling tightly, having forgotten how Cade could fill a room, making it feel small and other people seem boring. But it wasn't just his height and size that made him stand out. It was his intensity and his focus. When Cade King wanted something, he got it through sheer force of will.

And once upon a time, he'd wanted her.

But then later, he'd also wanted booze, and he'd been one of those guys who drank hard and often, and it worried her and scared her. And so she put it all on the line, wanting what was best for him, for them, and told him he needed to get sober or she couldn't stay. And he chose the booze over her.

"Everything else okay, though?" he asked, shifting on the yellow couch, almost crushing the cellophane-wrapped roses.

She nodded, determined to show no chink in her armor. "Yes. Very well," she said. The antique clock on the mantel chimed. She glanced at the pale gold face of the German-made clock, Grandma's prized possession. Her father, Rachel's great-grandfather, had brought the clock with him when he'd emigrated from Germany. It'd been a wedding present to Grandma and Grandpa when they'd married and it still kept time perfectly.

Four-thirty.

Which reminded her, she'd have to go get Tommy soon from Mrs. Munoz. She had fifteen minutes. Give or take a few.

Cade saw her glance at the clock. "Am I keeping you?"

"No, not yet. But I do need to leave in a few minutes. I have an appointment."

Rachel didn't know why she called it an appointment.

She was only picking Tommy up from his babysitter, but for some reason, she couldn't bring herself to mention Tommy. Not because she was ashamed of being a single, unwed mother, but because people had been so unkind about him and she'd learned to be protective.

"I won't keep you, then," Cade said, picking up the bouquet and standing. "It was good seeing you."

"It was good seeing you, too," she lied, determined to hang on to her composure to the very end, because it wasn't good seeing him. It was terrible. Painful. She couldn't handle seeing Cade. He made her feel things she didn't want to feel, made her remember a time in her life when everything had seemed hopeful and beautiful.

"I'll just put these in the kitchen," he said, his grip crinkling the cellophane on the flowers. He headed out of the cramped living room without waiting for a reply.

It wasn't until Cade was in the hall and moving toward the kitchen that he exhaled. Why had he come? It was a mistake to have come by, an even bigger mistake to have just dropped in on her unannounced. If he wanted to know how she was doing, he should have just called. Sent a letter. A text. An email. Anything but this.

Seeing her made it all too real. Made her damn real again, and that's the last thing he needed.

Getting her out of his system had taken *years*.

Entering Sally's old kitchen, he froze. An enormous, white, tiered wedding cake filled the old oak table, making the kitchen smell sugary and sweet. His gaze moved to the clear plastic box of flowers on the counter. It was a small floral bouquet of white, cream and pale pink flowers…

A wedding cake. A bridal bouquet. Cade swallowed hard, stunned. Rachel was getting married.

He felt her come up behind him and, glancing over his

shoulder, he saw her hovering in the doorway. "That's a lot of white cake," he said.

She smiled faintly, color turning her cheeks pink. "Better be. It has to feed over two hundred and forty people."

"Two hundred and forty?" he repeated.

"It was hard to narrow the guest list to that. It's a small town. Everyone wanted to go."

Of course everybody did, he thought, his chest tight and growing tighter. Mineral Wells was a small town and Sally James had been widely loved by all.

Cade glanced down at the tips of his boots, wishing yet again he'd never come. He'd wanted to know that Rachel was happy, but this…this wasn't how he wanted to see her… the blushing bride…the day before her wedding. But he had to be happy for her. This was what he wanted for her. Good things. Good people.

He forced himself to look up at her and he managed a smile. "Well, it's a beautiful cake with all that fancy lace. Have never seen that done before."

"The lace is actually icing. It's all edible."

"Really?"

"Yep," she answered, a hint of laughter in her eyes, and he felt a tug of emotion. There was no one prettier than Rachel James when she smiled.

"And it tastes good, too?"

"I think so. Mia called it heavenly."

"When is the wedding?"

"Tomorrow."

He was determined to be happy for her. He was. "Where?"

"Clark Gardens. Over in Weatherford."

He nodded and turned away to look out the kitchen window into her backyard. Cardboard boxes leaned against the garage. She'd been packing, getting ready for her move to her new life. "So you're happy?" he asked, not trusting himself to look at her, afraid of what she'd see in his eyes.

But she wasn't looking at him. She'd followed his gaze outside to the boxes. "Yes."

"I'm glad," he said, and then hesitated, wondering how to say the rest, wishing the words were easy, but they weren't easy, they'd never be easy. Best thing he could do was just say them. Straight out. "I'm sorry, Rachel, truly sorry for all the pain I caused you—"

"That was five years ago, Cade—"

"Maybe. But I was wrong. I was a selfish ass, and I ask your forgiveness—"

"Cade."

"Please, Rachel, forgive me."

"I do," she whispered. "I did. A long, long time ago."

He exhaled and glanced around the kitchen, still able to see them all here. Sally, Rachel and him, having dinner, lingering over dessert, teasing and talking and telling stories. Sally had a nice dining-room set, but she preferred the kitchen table. He did, too, and he'd cherished those meals in here. They were warm and real and special. And he felt like one of those kids on TV who'd grown up with a normal family, a nice family...

"Things have worked out the way they were meant to," she added kindly.

He nodded, his gut cramping, his chest hot and tight. He was glad she was happy. Glad everything in her world was good. "You deserve every good thing, Rachel," he said, placing the flowers gently on the table. "You really do."

And then he was walking out of there, fast, needing to escape the little house and all its memories before he said or did something stupid.

Chapter Two

Cade shoved his hat onto his head as he headed to his truck, his boots thudding against the pavement.

That had been a disaster. His timing couldn't have been worse. Showing up on her doorstep the day before her wedding? Awesome. It was bad enough seeing the fancy cake and hearing the ceremony details. Thank God he hadn't caught her in her actual wedding gown. That would have pushed him over the edge.

Starting his truck, he pulled away from the ranch house, his gut churning as he drove.

Hot, sharp emotions surged within him. Emotions he hadn't felt in God knew how long. Disappointment and regret, but relief, too. Relief that she was okay. Relief that she was cared for. Not by him—which hurt—but by someone better. Because Cade King might be a champion on the rodeo circuit, but he was no prince in real life. He had problems…issues…for God's sake, he was an alcoholic.

True, he hadn't had a drink in over two years, and he continued to go to his AA meetings, even when he was traveling, but once an alcoholic, always an alcoholic. You could put *recovering* or *recovered* before the word *alcoholic,* but it still meant the same thing.

Cade exhaled, trying to ease some of the pressure in his chest, but his deep breaths did nothing to ease the ache.

That was his girl, back there. His woman. And it was damn hard to walk away from your woman, even if it was the right thing.

But she was okay, he reminded himself. Better than okay. She was happy and in love and getting married tomorrow. Everything had worked out for her. And while the way he left her would never be right, at least she'd found someone who would treat her the way she deserved to be treated—like a princess. No, make that a queen.

Cade glanced at the clock on his dash. He still had an hour and a half before his appointment with Jeffrey Farms, a horse farm that was interested in using Cade's stallion Orion as a stud. Adam Jeffrey had offered to come to him, but Cade had been thinking about Rachel lately—couldn't get her out of his mind these past few months—and he'd thought that by coming to Mineral Wells he could kill two birds with one stone. Meet Adam, discuss the stud fee. See Rachel, make sure she was fine. Go home, business accomplished, mind at ease.

And his mind should be at ease. His conscience could rest easy. But his heart sure felt like hell.

He'd always thought he'd be the one to marry her. From the moment they met, he'd known she was the one for him. And it might have been five years ago, but he still remembered the day they first met as clear as anything.

He'd been crossing the street in downtown Mineral Wells and a girl on a bike—one of those old-fashioned bikes with a big wicker basket attached to the handlebars—turned the corner and crashed into him. He'd been surprised but unhurt. But she, and her bike, had gone flying, straight into the curb.

Cars slammed on brakes, and between the screech of brakes and rubber tires squealing, he'd rushed to get her out of the street.

"I'm sorry," she said, as he scooped her up into his arms. "I didn't see you. I'm so sorry—"

"It's all right," he said.

She shoved dark glossy hair from her eyes. "No, it's not. I could have killed you—"

He laughed. He couldn't help it. "No, you couldn't have," he said, stepping onto the sidewalk and glancing down at her. She was bleeding everywhere—her cheek and chin, her elbows and knees—but thankfully, nothing looked broken.

"Yes, I could," she retorted irritably, looking up into his eyes. "Cyclists kill pedestrians all the time."

Her fine dark brows had pulled, and she looked so cross and serious that his lips had twitched, fighting a grin. "How 'bout you? You okay?" he asked.

"Yes," she said, dabbing her cheek where she'd skinned it. "And you can put me down. I'm tough. I'm not your average girl."

He'd held her a moment longer, just because he could, and then gently he'd placed her on her feet, keeping a close eye on her in case she wobbled. But she didn't.

"See?" she demanded.

"Not your average girl," he agreed.

And then she laughed, her light gray eyes crinkling at the corners. Her eyes looked so cool and clear, they made him think of a summer rain. He'd stared into her eyes trying to find the bottom.

She let him look, too. She let him drink her in as if she were a refreshing glass of ice water on a humid afternoon. Until he soaked her in, he hadn't realized how thirsty he had been.

No, he thought, she wasn't his average girl. She was far from average, could never be average, not in her faded yellow cotton sundress, the soft mustard-hued fabric sprigged with blue flowers, the neckline edged with tired lace. It wasn't just because she was pretty—there was something else in her that called to him. Something about her that felt right…familiar and new, exciting, terrifying, but also right. Looking down into her light gray eyes he suddenly knew why he'd left home at fifteen to find his way in the world. He knew why he'd been through hell and back. It was for her, this girl. To love her and protect her and keep her safe…

He'd put her bike into the back of his truck and driven her home, and he'd returned the next day to check on her, and her grandmother had invited him to stay for dinner. And he'd returned for dinner every night that he wasn't on the road, competing.

But later his demons caught up with him, and what started out as a drink now and then turned to drinking 24/7, and all of Cade's good intentions were drowned out by his need for Jack Daniel's.

Once in one of his AA meetings, after he'd shared his story, someone said to him, "Thank God you sobered up before you hurt someone," and Cade had nearly puked right there in the middle of the church basement where the meeting was being held. Because he had hurt someone. He'd trashed Rachel. And maybe it wasn't a drinking and driving accident, but it was just as destructive. Maybe even more so because it was personal.

NEEDING TO KILL TIME, CADE stopped for dinner downtown in his favorite diner. It was still early, almost five, but the place was half-full with seniors who'd come in for the early-bird special.

Cade ordered coffee and chicken fried steak with mashed potatoes, then picked up a paper somebody had left behind in another booth and sat back down to read while he waited for his food. He scanned the headlines before flipping to the business section, checking the agriculture report and then the NASDAQ to see where his stock closed the day before.

His dinner arrived before he finished reading the business section, so he folded the paper and continued to read as he ate.

Midway through his meal, a strong hand clapped his shoulder. "Cade King, it's been a while. How are you? What brings you back to Mineral Wells?"

Cade pushed his plate away and wiped his mouth as he looked up at Larry Strauss, a burly rancher in his early sixties. He smiled warily and extended his hand, knowing that Larry was close family friends with the Jameses. "It has been a while," he agreed. "Care to join me? Do you have time?"

"I've already eaten but I will sit for a minute." Larry slid into the booth seat across from Cade. "Quite a year you've had, son. Third straight All-Around title in a row, isn't it?"

"Yes, sir. I've been lucky."

"That's not luck, that's skill. And you won easily this year."

"I drew some good bulls. Two of them were yours."

The older rancher inclined his head. Strauss Ranch was known on the circuit for their outstanding rough stock, including their bucking bulls. "But you knew what to do with them, and that's what counts." He gestured to the waitress that he'd have a cup of coffee, too. "So what brings you to town?" His narrowed gaze raked over Cade, his expression a little less friendly. "Haven't seen you in years."

Cade noted the coolness in Larry's tone. He wasn't surprised. Larry would have known that Cade had callously given Rachel the boot, and Larry being the old-fashioned rancher he was, wouldn't have liked it. "Haven't been back in years," he answered evenly. "But I'm meeting with one of the Jeffrey brothers from Jeffrey Farms a little later. They're interested in one of my horses."

"Have you stayed in touch with any of the folks here?"

Cade knew exactly what Larry was asking, and he shifted on the vinyl booth. "Not the way I should have."

"Did you hear that Sally James passed a couple years ago?"

"Found out today."

"She was a good woman."

"Yes, she was," Cade agreed. There were few people he'd liked as much as he'd liked Sally. She was born to nurture, and she'd been kinder to him than any of the foster-care mothers he'd known in his seven and a half years under the state's care.

"Rachel took her passing hard," Larry added, glancing up, staring Cade straight in the eyes.

Cade nodded. "I can imagine."

Larry's light blue eyes bored into his. "She hasn't had an easy life."

"Who?"

"Rachel."

Gut knotting, Cade stretched his legs out under the table. "She seems like she's doing all right now."

"Have you seen her?"

"Yes. Today. Stopped by the house. Thought she looked great. Thinner, but still the prettiest girl in Texas."

"So you know what's going on with her?"

"She told me."

Larry looked skeptical. "Doesn't bother you?"

Cade shrugged uneasily. He didn't want to talk about Rachel, or think about her getting married tomorrow. He was glad for her. He was. But it didn't give him cause for celebration. "Things didn't work out the way we'd imagined, but that's life. You don't always get what you want."

Larry's bushy gray eyebrows lifted. "Wouldn't have pegged you for heartless, King."

"Not heartless, just realistic. Things don't always go as planned. So you move on and, frankly, things have worked out the way they were meant to be."

"You sound like the rest of them, judging her. But everybody makes mistakes and Lord knows, she's had her hands full. First with Tommy, then Sally's cancer—"

"You're misunderstanding me. I'm not judging her. I'm happy for her. Happy that things have turned out the way they have for her."

"Which part makes you happy, son?" Larry asked slowly, dragging the words out.

Cade's right hand clenched into a fist under the table. What was the point of this? What did Larry want from him? "I'm glad she's found happiness—"

"You're joking, right?"

Cade drew a sharp, deep breath. "Why would I joke about something like that? I care about Rachel, and I'm happy she's getting married tomorrow, and I hope he's a great guy. He better be a great guy—"

"Rachel's not getting married tomorrow."

"Yes, she is. We talked about it, and she showed me the flowers and the cake."

Larry laughed shortly. "Rachel showed you a cake because she's a baker. She supports herself by making cakes, works out of her home, and this cake was for *Mia,* who is getting married tomorrow afternoon over in Weatherford at the botanical gardens, *not* Rachel."

The cake was for Mia…

It was Mia getting married, not Rachel…

Cade's brain worked to process this information but it didn't make sense, and he found himself frowning, feeling stupid. Something wasn't right. "If Rachel's not getting married, why is she moving?"

Larry didn't immediately answer. Instead he took a big sip from his coffee cup and then slowly set the cup back down in the saucer, his expression hard and scornful as he met Cade's troubled gaze. Silence stretched, heavy with disapproval. "Maybe, cowboy, you should ask her."

RACHEL MOVED SOUNDLESSLY through her house, picking up a few toys, turning out a table lamp in the living room, washing up Tommy's dessert plate and cup from his milk.

Tommy had fallen asleep earlier tonight than usual, but frankly, it was a good thing. He'd come home from Mrs. Munoz overly exhausted, stressed and needing to decompress, which for him meant opening and closing his bedroom door thirty some times. She'd tried to distract him, but it'd only made him more determined to bang, so after a while she left him to his door activity. She folded a load of laundry, and then unloaded the dishwasher, trying to stay busy, trying to stay calm, trying not to worry about Tommy or think about Cade.

But now Tommy was in bed, and the house was tidy, and the laundry put away, and she couldn't keep Cade from intruding on her thoughts any longer.

Cade had once been her world. She'd loved him so much, and she knew he wasn't perfect, knew he had his fair share of demons…not that he talked about them. No, Cade was private and a bit of a lone wolf. But he'd loved her and Grandma. He'd really loved Grandma, and her grandmother had loved him, too.

She opened a flat empty box and was taping the bottom when the doorbell rang. Rachel tore the tape, sealed the flaps and hurried to the front door, hoping that the doorbell wouldn't wake up Tommy. Wondering who'd be stopping by now, Rachel peeked through the window and saw a big black pickup truck with a huge cab and lots of shiny chrome parked out front. Rachel dropped the curtain, tensing. Cade's truck.

He was back.

Stomach knotting, she unlocked the front door. "Cade," she said, opening the door.

His head tipped. "Rachel."

Her heart was racing, thudding so hard her hands shook, and suddenly she couldn't do this. Make conversation with him again. Act as though everything was all right. Everything wasn't all right. She was exhausted, frazzled and overwhelmed, and seeing him just made it worse. Seeing him made her realize how much life had happened in the past five-plus years. How much had happened to her. She'd changed. She wasn't the same girl he'd left behind, and there was no place in her life for him now.

And so instead of letting him into the house, she stepped out onto the porch, quietly closing the door behind her, not wanting to wake Tommy. But joining Cade on the small stoop put her in close proximity with him, reminding her with a jolt that he wasn't just tall, but broad shouldered, lean hipped and handsome. Heartbreakingly handsome. But looks had never been his problem. Drinking was his problem. Drinking and control…or lack of.

But she didn't want to go there, didn't want to feel all that again. Deliberately she pushed the past away and glanced out to the street where the lamp shone yellow on Cade's big glossy truck. "That's a nice truck."

"Bought it two years ago with some of the prize money, and now it's got close to 100,000 miles on it."

"You do a lot of driving."

"That I do." He hesitated, cleared his throat. "Just saw Larry Strauss. At the diner downtown."

"How's he?" she asked, crossing her arms tightly over her chest to keep from shivering. It was a clear night and cold, but she wasn't going to be out here long enough to need a sweater.

"Good." Cade paused. "But concerned about you."

"Oh? Why?"

"He said you're moving."

"I'm not allowed to move?"

"But this was your grandmother's house, and your house—"

"Not anymore."

"She didn't leave it to you?"

"No, Grandma did."

"Then why would—"

Cade never finished. He couldn't because he was cut off by a piercing shriek from inside the house.

Rachel threw open the door, racing inside to Tommy, who stood in the middle of the hallway in his pajamas.

"Ma! Ma!" he screamed, even as she crouched in front of him.

"Hey, Tommy, Momma's here. It's okay." She tried to smooth his dark hair back from his forehead but he flinched and pulled away.

"Ma." He batted her hand away.

"Did you have a bad dream?"

But he wasn't listening to her. He was looking past her to Cade, who'd followed Rachel inside.

"Man," he said, staring at Cade.

She glanced over her shoulder, her stomach falling. Cade's jaw had dropped. He looked stunned. She swallowed hard, wishing none of this was happening. "That's Mommy's friend. Cade. Cade King."

Tommy shook his head. He didn't like strangers, and he especially didn't like them in his home. "Go."

"Tommy, can you say hi to Mr. King?"

"Man. Go. Leave."

"That's not nice," she rebuked gently, reaching up and trying once again to soothe him by smoothing a fistful of hair off his brow. This time he let her, and her palm lingered on top of his head, his hair silky smooth and reminding her of rich, dark chocolate.

"Leave," he insisted, pointing at Cade. "Go. Leave." Then he pushed her hand away and ran back to his room.

Rachel watched him go, heart heavy, before standing and looking at Cade, her lips curving in a tight smile. "And that was my son, Thomas James." Her gaze met Cade's and held. "And no, he's not yours. He's four and a half. He'll be five in July."

Then she, too, walked away, but headed in the opposite direction, going to her kitchen where she pushed in the chairs around the small kitchen table, the legs scraping the old linoleum floor, and knocked an imaginary crumb off the scratched table surface.

Cade entered the kitchen, too, but she ignored him, continuing to straighten things that didn't need straightening, but it was better than looking at Cade and seeing whatever it was he was thinking.

"He has developmental delays," she said jerkily, adjusting the faded terry-cloth dish towel hanging on the handle fronting the old oven. "Autism. Which isn't actually a single disorder, but a spectrum of closely related disorders—" She broke off, took another breath. "And he doesn't mean to be rude. He just doesn't have strong verbal skills."

"That's all right."

She heard his flat tone and shot Cade a quick glance. He looked pale, almost sick, and she looked away just as swiftly. It'd been so difficult getting Tommy diagnosed... none of the Mineral Wells doctors agreed on his exact diagnosis. Obviously Tommy had PDD, pervasive developmental disorder, but was it classical autism or autism with Asperger's syndrome, or PDD-NOS? "People don't understand that he has special needs. He's not a bad boy, and he's not a problem. He just gets agitated easily. Overwhelmed by change and too much stimuli. Kind of a sensory overload."

"You don't have to explain to me. I wouldn't judge him or criticize him."

Her head jerked up again, and her eyes searched his. She knew Cade had had problems, knew he'd gotten in plenty of trouble growing up, and wished she could believe him. But she didn't. Couldn't. Her shoulders twisted. "You wouldn't like how he acts in public. You'd say he was out of control. And you know, he does get out of control. He'll throw something in a store—a can of soup or frozen orange juice—and it'll hit someone or something, or he'll knock over a display and send a hundred packages of toilet paper all over the store. And you'd be like everyone else. 'Why don't you give that boy some discipline?' It's embarrassing, but it's not his fault. He didn't ask to be born this way—" She stopped, gasping for breath, horrified to discover she was close to tears. "Sorry. I'm sorry. I'm tired. It's been a long day."

Cade didn't say anything and after a long moment Rachel glanced at him. He was leaning against one of the counters, big arms bracing his weight, his jaw set, his brow furrowed, his gaze resting on the cardboard box she'd just begun to pack, looking every inch the bull-riding champion he was. Not just All-Around champion, but a bull-riding champion, too. In the past seven years he'd won four national bull-riding titles in one of the world's most dangerous sports. *Four.* The man was fearless. Tough as nails. Stronger than anyone she'd ever met, but also more dangerous, too.

"Where's his dad?" he asked roughly.

"Not in the picture."

"Why not?"

She drew a ragged breath. "His dad didn't want him."

Cade was slow to respond and hot emotion rolled through her, blistering her heart. "But that's okay," she said fiercely, "because I do. And I love him. I love him more than anything in this world and he is perfect to me. Absolutely perfect and just the way God intended him to be."

His lips curved but his eyes were shadowed. "I bet Sally doted on him," he said quietly.

Rachel blinked back tears. "Loved him to pieces."

He nodded once, as if thinking. "So if Sally left you the house, and this is where you're raising your boy, why are you moving, Rache?" he asked, looking up at her, his voice gentle.

"I couldn't pay the property taxes." There, she'd said it. Now he knew. She didn't feel much better, but the truth was out in the open. "So we lost the house."

"The taxes couldn't have been much—"

"Grandma had deferred taxes for eight years, and even though it's deferred, you're accumulating interest and fines, and a little bit of money turns into a lot of money. By the time it was brought to my attention…" Her voice faded and she shook her head, sickened all over again by her inability to save her home. "It was too late."

"Let me pay the taxes for you, Rachel."

Of course this was what he'd say. This had always been Cade's way. Cade was generous to a fault, and she knew he'd help her. Cade liked helping people. Cade had once loved being the good guy…rushing in, playing hero, being Mr. Wonderful—and he was Mr. Wonderful, he could be incredibly wonderful—until he started craving his buddy Jack Daniel's again. "You can't," she said huskily. "I don't own the house anymore. That's why we're moving."

"Who bought the house? And how much did they pay you for it?"

She blinked, but couldn't hide the tears. "Some company in Fort Worth bought it. But they didn't pay me—they paid the county. Turns out all they had to do was go in and pay all the back taxes on Grandma's house, and the house became theirs." She put a hand to her mouth, fighting to hang on to her composure. And then when she was sure she could speak without falling apart, she added, "That's why we're moving. Another family is moving in middle of the month."

"So they got Sally's house for what…twenty-five thousand? Thirty?"

"Twenty and some change." She laughed even as she cried, because it was ludicrous—it was. And Larry Strauss had offered to help her. Mia's parents had wanted to help her. Even Mrs. Munoz had tried to give her some money but she couldn't take it. Not from any of them. She was proud, and it was a fault of hers, but she couldn't bear to go through life pitied and whispered and talked about. It was better to lose the house and maintain some self-respect, than take loans from people she'd never be able to pay back.

"You told me earlier today that everything had worked out the way things were meant to work out." Cade's voice was hard. "But that's not true—"

"Yes, it is." Rachel jerked her chin up. "I have Tommy and I love being a mom and I wouldn't have it any other way."

Chapter Three

Cade drove the deserted back roads to his ranch as if the devil pursued him. It was reckless driving, but then his thoughts were reckless, too. Fortunately it was late, and the moon was high, casting bright winter light across the dark pastures and clusters of oak and elm trees.

Cade knew these back roads well, and he drove with his foot heavy on the accelerator. With its V-8 engine, his truck could fly and it flew now.

He'd told himself five years ago he was leaving her for the right reasons. He'd told himself he was walking because he wanted a different life…a better life than the one he had with Rachel.

But it wasn't true.

He'd walked away from her out of laziness. Selfishness. He'd left her because he hadn't wanted to change. He'd left to send her a message that he wasn't about to let her start controlling him. He'd had enough of that growing up, being bounced around from home to home in foster care, and he was done being dictated to. Done having people tell him who he was supposed to be and how he was supposed to behave. Done being criticized and marginalized. He was a man and he was going to succeed his way, on his terms.

And so he left Rachel, sure that it'd been the right thing to do—for her, and himself—and for the next couple of

years he'd lived his life his way…drinking too much sometimes, getting some success on the circuit, winning some big
events only to lose others. He was always hurt or rehabilitat-
ing—part of the life of a professional rodeo cowboy—and
alcohol helped ease the pain. He drank to medicate himself.
Drank to help himself sleep. Drank to help himself forget.

But drunk, he thought of Rachel. Sober, he thought of
Rachel.

Rachel became his demon, and he vowed he'd excise his
demon once and for all.

And he thought he had, until he'd sat in one of those
damn AA meetings two years ago November and thought
about the people he'd hurt with his drinking, and Rachel was
top of the list. But she was the one person he couldn't go
to. The one person he couldn't face. Not because she didn't
deserve an apology, but because he didn't want to see her.

Didn't want to be reminded of what he'd lost.

But it ate at him over the months…ate at him through the
holidays and the New Year and all through this past year
until the holidays rolled around again.

What if she wasn't okay?

What if she needed something?

What if she needed someone?

He didn't know why he couldn't relax. He was sure she'd
be fine. Rachel was smart and pretty as anything. What
man wouldn't sweep her off her feet and give her the sto-
rybook happy ending?

But the thing was he didn't know for sure, and he needed
to know, with the need for knowledge and a resolution becoming stronger with every passing day until he traveled
to Mineral Wells to see her for himself.

And now he saw, and he knew, and he'd been wrong.

So very, very wrong.

She wasn't okay. And sure, she could make light of losing
her house—Sally's house—and she could be brave about

raising a little boy with developmental disorders on her own, but he knew the truth. He knew how her story was supposed to go, and it wasn't like this.

Acid burned his belly. He longed to lean out the window and puke. To vomit all the pain out of his body. But it wouldn't help the pain in his heart.

Cade couldn't remember the last time he felt so ill.

That wasn't true. He could remember. Five and a half years ago in a moment of alcohol-induced righteousness, he told himself he didn't need a nineteen-year-old girl giving him an ultimatum, and he'd climbed out of bed, stepped into his jeans and his boots and walked out on her.

Cade blinked. His eyes felt gritty. Hot. He blinked again, trying to clear his vision. The gate to his property came into view and he braked, punching the remote in his truck that opened the gate.

Pulling through his gate, his vision clouded again. His lashes felt damp. Cade ground his teeth together, his jaw aching at the effort to restrain emotion. Leaving Rachel had hurt, but not half as much as knowing how much he'd wounded her.

IT'D BEEN A ROUGH NIGHT and a rough morning, Rachel thought, watching the tow-truck driver pull away from her and her broken-down car, leaving them both on the side of the road where the driver had found them. And now things weren't merely bad, they were the worst.

As in the worst-case scenario.

Mia's wedding was supposed to start any minute, and yet Mia's gorgeous wedding cake was still in Rachel's car—a fifteen-year-old Jeep Cherokee she'd bought secondhand but was ideal for transporting cakes—because the tow-truck driver couldn't hitch the Jeep to his truck without destroying the cake, and there was no way Rachel was going to let Mia get married without her cake.

In between calling the tow-truck company and waiting
for the driver to arrive, she'd phoned a half-dozen different
people trying to find someone who could transport the cake
to the gardens in Weatherford, but no one was answering
and she knew why. They were all at the wedding.

My God. This couldn't be happening. It couldn't.

If there was one small blessing it's that Tommy was with
Mrs. Munoz for the afternoon and wasn't here to see her
fall apart.

But no, she couldn't fall apart, not yet, not until the cake
was delivered to the gardens.

Staring out toward the highway, her heart thumping a
mile a minute, she suddenly thought of Cade's black truck.
His truck would be perfect. It had a huge cab and plenty of
space for a delicate four-layer wedding cake.

Rachel didn't know where Cade lived anymore, only that
he had a ranch somewhere in Parker County, and Weatherford was the seat of Parker County, so he couldn't be that
far out of the way…

It'd been over five years since she'd tried to call him,
but she knew his old cell number, would always know that
number, and wondered if it would work now.

Quickly she punched in the number and held her breath,
praying it was the right number, praying he'd answer, praying he was free—

"Hello?"

Her stomach fell and her legs turned to jelly. "Cade?"
she whispered.

"Rachel? What's wrong?"

Of course he knew that if she called him something had
happened. He, of all people, would realize this wasn't a social call. Overwhelmed by intensely ambivalent emotions,
she couldn't speak for a moment, her throat swelling closed.

"Rache?"

"I'm okay. I'm just…" She glanced around her at the
fields bordering the empty highway. It was a very rural

highway with minimal traffic this time of day. "…stuck on the side of 180 with Mia's cake in back of my Jeep. I can deal with my car later, but I've got to get Mia's cake to the reception—"

"I'm on my way."

He reached her in twenty-eight minutes. Rachel knew because she'd stared at the clock on her phone the entire time, and then once he arrived, in dark dress jeans and a black jacket that matched his black hat, he had the enormous cake out of the cargo area of her Jeep and into the cab of his truck in no time. She didn't even have to tell him to be careful. He handled her cake as if it were made of glass. Arriving at the gardens, Cade summoned the catering staff and put them to work, moving the cake into its spot on the round table near the dance floor just as the first guests began to stream into the tent.

Without even shedding her coat, Rachel went to work repairing some of the little buttercream swags and re-creating some of the torn lacework with the tubes of icing she'd brought from home. She stood back to inspect her handiwork. It wasn't perfect but it was still damn good and Mia would never notice.

Heaving a massive sigh of relief that the cake was here and safe and beautiful, Rachel quickly tucked the tubes of icing back into her bag, hiding them from the guests who'd begun to wander around the tent looking for their places at their assigned tables.

She glanced up to discover Cade watching her, a curious expression in his blue eyes. "What?" she asked him.

"You're amazing."

She blushed and pushed a wave of dark hair from her warm cheek. "Perhaps you haven't been paying attention, but I'm actually something of a disaster."

"I have been paying attention, and you have no idea

how much you impress me. You're a beautiful and amazing woman, Rachel James."

A lump formed in her throat and she had to blink and look away. There was a time when she'd hung on to his every word, when a compliment from Cade made her float on the air. But now his compliments stung because they were just words, and she didn't trust words, and she definitely didn't trust him.

"Maybe we could find something cold to drink," she said. "I'm really thirsty. How about you?"

CADE HAD PROMISED RACHEL that he'd drive her back to Mineral Wells whenever she was ready to leave the reception, and Rachel had warned him that it wouldn't be until after the cake was cut, in case there was a cake emergency. But fortunately for Mia—and Rachel—there was no cake emergency, and at four the cake was finally cut and devoured. In fact, not a piece remained anywhere, including the small top round, which Mia had intended to save.

When told that Mia was near tears over losing the smallest cake round, Rachel found Mia in the ladies' room dabbing her eye makeup, and Rachel gave her a quick hug. "Don't cry," Rachel begged her. "I'm going to make you a miniature wedding cake for your first wedding anniversary next year. It will be just as lovely and will taste twice as good, since it will be fresh and not frozen for a year."

Mia blinked as new tears welled. "Really? You'd do that for me?"

"Yes." Rachel grinned and winked. "It's a piece of cake."

Now buttoning up her winter coat, Rachel walked with Cade through the gardens on their way to his truck. "That was such a beautiful wedding," Rachel said, her high heels crunching gravel as they left the paved path for the parking lot. "But it's always a relief when the cake has been cut and eaten, and I know the bride and groom were happy."

"I heard you promised to make Mia a small cake for her wedding anniversary," Cade said, fishing his keys from his pocket.

"She was so sad that the top round was eaten and there's no reason for her to be sad today. It's simple enough for me to make her something for next year."

He opened the passenger-side door of his truck for her. "Will you charge her for the anniversary cake?" he asked, offering her his hand to give her a boost up.

"No."

"I didn't think so," he said, closing the door behind her and walking around the truck to climb into the driver's seat.

Rachel watched him settle behind the steering wheel. He was such a big, solid man. Even in a truck this size, he seemed to completely fill the cab. "What does that mean?"

"Just that you are exactly who you've always been. Loyal, loving, generous."

"She's my friend. I'm a professional baker. It's the least I can do."

He shifted in his seat, his lips curving faintly. "Darlin', I'm not criticizing you. I'm complimenting you. I respect you and admire you. You're a good woman, through and through." His smile slipped, faded, and he reached out to smooth a dark tendril of hair from her face. "And I didn't know your parents, but I heard your grandma talk about them plenty, and I can tell you this, if they were alive, they'd be very proud of you, too."

For a long time Rachel couldn't speak, too overwhelmed by emotions to say anything. But when they reached the place she'd left her car on Highway 180 and discovered it was gone, she looked at Cade. "My Jeep?"

"I had it towed to a good mechanic in Mineral Wells." He suddenly sounded uncertain. "Hope that's okay?"

She glanced at him and took in his creased forehead and troubled gaze. "Yes. I appreciate the help, and I appreciate you driving me home." She hesitated. "You remember we've got to stop at Tommy's sitter on the way, too, right?"

"I do."

They both fell silent and they drove for nearly ten minutes without talking before Cade broke the silence. "I'm sorry, Rachel. I really am."

"It's fine," she said quickly.

"No, it's not," he answered brusquely. "It's anything but okay, and we both know it."

The curtness of his tone surprised her and she glanced at him in the dim light of the cab interior. It had been twilight when they'd left the wedding but it was nearly dark outside now, which made it hard to read his expression. "It was a long time ago, Cade."

"Not that long ago. I remember."

Rachel pressed her lips together, her insides suddenly bruised and too tender.

"I remember the drinking," he added tersely. "I remember the fights and the tears. I remember you crying—"

"Cade." She cut him short, pressing her hands to her knees, her voice strangled, because she remembered, too.

"I remember you telling me how much you loved me, and that I was everything."

She closed her eyes, steeling herself against the past, against the terrible ache, as well as the scar covering her heart, which barely held it together. "Let's not do this," she said, thinking he had no idea how hard it had been to get over him and even harder to accept that once he left, he wasn't coming back.

"Rachel, I remember our last night together. We were

in bed and you had your arms around me and your cheek pressed to my chest, and your tears were falling on my bare skin. I remember how hot they felt as they fell."

She angled her body away from him and stared out the truck window, her fist pressed to her mouth to keep from making a sound, because every detail from that last night was permanently engraved in her memory. It was the night she gave him the ultimatum. It was time he got help. Time he stopped drinking. She loved him so much, but she couldn't stand by and watch him self-destruct.

And he'd listened to her that night, quiet, so very, very quiet and much too still, and then after an endless silence that stretched for fifteen minutes, then thirty, he smoothed his hand over her head and kissed her forehead and said she was right. She was absolutely right. She did deserve better. Then he climbed from bed, stepped into his jeans and dressed. And left.

He left her.

She waited days, weeks, months for him to come back. Waited days, weeks, months for him to come to his senses, remember how much he loved her, remember how she was his heart and his life and his soul. Waited for him to be the man he'd always said he'd be for her.

But he didn't return.

Didn't call, didn't write, didn't email, didn't do anything and Grandma kept telling her to give him time…give him time…but it was killing her, not hearing from him, killing her, not knowing how he was doing and what he was doing… killing her that he could have forgotten her so completely. And so she tracked him down, showing up in Waco where he'd entered a rodeo, hoping that once he saw her, he'd remember how much he loved her. But it didn't work out that way. He saw her, all right, but she saw him, too, lip-locked on the rodeo grounds with another brunette. Rachel's replacement.

Rachel met David a week later while out with girlfriends in Fort Worth. Her friends had dragged her with them for a girls' night out, determined to help her forget Cade. They'd driven to Fort Worth and gone line dancing. David was there that night at the bar, and he'd been handsome and charming. He had bought her drinks and all of her friends drinks, and showered her with compliments.

Rachel didn't normally fall for guys like David—a little too smooth, a little too polished, a little too quick with a line—but he made her feel special and important, and desperate to get over Cade, Rachel slept with him on the second date—just that once—because they never went out again, but Rachel only needed that one time to get pregnant.

David didn't want anything to do with her or the baby when she told him. He even moved to Calgary, taking a job there, to make sure he couldn't be roped into anything.

Thank God Grandma had been there. Thank God Grandma had loved her. She drew another quick, painful breath and then forced herself to face Cade. "You want to talk about this? Okay, fine, we'll talk. Yes, the way you left me hurt. But I'm not mad at you, Cade, and to be perfectly honest, I don't think about you, either. I have Tommy now, and he's my life, and I wouldn't have had him if you and I had stayed together."

Chapter Four

When they arrived at Mrs. Munoz's small house in Mineral Wells, Cade put the truck into Park, and Rachel opened the passenger door and headed up the front walk to get Tommy.

Rachel thought Mrs. Munoz looked pale and tired as she handed over Tommy's small backpack and his coat. "Everything go okay today?" Rachel asked her sitter as she crouched in front of Tommy, zipping up his puffy winter jacket.

"Everything was fine." Mrs. Munoz leaned on the back of a chair in the hall. "He was a good boy. I'm just not feeling so well."

In the four years that Rachel had known Mrs. Munoz, Mrs. Munoz had never once complained about anything and Rachel swiftly straightened, concerned. "What's wrong?"

"It's probably nothing."

That was never a good sign, Rachel thought, forehead creasing. "Are you sick?"

"No, no. The doctor just wants to run some tests—"

"What kind of tests?"

"It's nothing. Don't worry about me."

"But I am worried, Mrs. Munoz. What kind of tests?"

"They want to check my heart, but it's probably nothing—"

"Oh, Mrs. Munoz, why didn't you tell me?"

"Because we don't know anything yet, and you need help—"

"But having Tommy here can't be good for you."

The elderly woman shrugged. "He likes coming here, and I like having him here."

Rachel's chest squeezed tight and she felt the pressure inside her grow, the old pressure she'd felt when Sally was dying and Rachel was eaten alive with guilt that her grandmother was exhausting herself trying to help her. She felt the same guilt now because Mrs. Munoz was a truly lovely woman and had been an invaluable help these past several years. Rachel wondered now if she'd leaned on the caregiver too much.

"When do you see the doctor again?" Rachel asked her.

"He wanted me to do the tests a couple weeks ago, but you've had those two weddings, and now the move—"

"My work and the move aren't more important than your health! Nothing is more important than your health, Mrs. Munoz, and I'm going to keep Tommy with me this week until you get your tests done and have your results and you know what's going on."

Rachel gave Mrs. Munoz a fierce hug goodbye, but walking to Cade's truck with Tommy's hand tucked in hers, Rachel felt close to tears. Mrs. Munoz was such a sweet lady. Nothing could happen to her. Nothing.

Fortunately, Tommy loved Cade's truck and was happy to be riding in the cab's backseat where he could play with the leather armrest with the built-in cup holder. But Rachel was nervous he might break the armrest by flipping it down too aggressively and cautioned him to be more gentle.

"It's okay," Cade told her. "He's not going to break anything."

"You don't know that. He does break things. Frequently."

Cade shrugged. "Then if he breaks it, I'll fix it. No big deal."

She opened her mouth to protest, and then blurted something completely different. "Tommy's babysitter, Mrs. Munoz, isn't well." Her voice cracked. "She might be having heart problems."

Cade shot her a swift look. "Does that put you in a bad spot?"

"I'm not worried about me. I'm worried about her. She's been wonderful to us…really loving and so patient with Tommy. She never gets mad at him, and whenever I'm in a bind she always comes through for me. And then she makes us homemade enchiladas and the best tamales at Christmas—" Rachel broke off as tears filled her eyes and she suddenly couldn't stop them. They fell in great fat warm drops and she reached up to catch them, but they were falling faster than she could wipe them away. "It just doesn't seem fair. I know we're mortal, but life is just so short, and the people I care about just keep going away—"

And then she stopped talking, embarrassed she'd said so much, and to Cade, of all people! He was the one who'd broken her heart into a thousand pieces and had made every loss after hurt worse.

"I'm sorry, Rachel," he said quietly, his voice pitched low.

She nodded, struggling to get control. Suddenly he reached out to her and placed his hand on her knee, his palm warm against her skin. From someone else the touch might have been sexual, but this wasn't sexual Cade, it was loving Cade, the Cade who knew her and had once been so good at comforting her.

At the house, Rachel unlocked the front door and then flipped on the entry light, before getting the hallway lights that led to the bedrooms. Tommy let out a yelp and pushed past her, running down the hall to eagerly turn on all the lights he could reach. He loved lights, and light switches, loved fans, too. Anything that could go on or off fascinated him for hours.

"Tommy's not afraid of the dark?" Cade asked, watching Tommy disappear down the hall.

"Not if he's the first one to turn the lights on. It's a game to him," Rachel answered wryly, still feeling a little raw from being so emotional on the way home. "But come in. I should go check on him."

Moving through the house, Rachel noted that Tommy had managed to turn every overhead light on in the three bedrooms and two bathrooms before throwing himself down on the floor of his room with his tub of LEGO. He was in the process of dumping the entire bin out when she looked in on him, but it was fine. Dumping out and picking up thousands of pieces of LEGO was a daily occurrence around here.

Smiling, she returned to the entry where Cade was waiting. "He's playing," she said, peeling her coat off and hanging it in the hall closet. "He'll be happy for a while, too. Once Tommy's engrossed in something, he's focused."

"Is this when you get some time to yourself?"

Rachel laughed. "Moms don't get time to themselves… not unless you call dinner, laundry and bills 'mom time.'" She glanced at her watch, saw that it was almost six. "Speaking of dinner, I'd better get something started because Tommy will be hungry soon."

"I'll head off, then."

"You don't have to. If you like frozen pizza, you're welcome to stay."

"Frozen pizza?" he repeated, not looking overly enthused.

Rachel laughed again, unable to help herself. "Or we can order pizza, but if we do that, you're paying."

"Done. Tell me what kind of pizza you guys like, and I'll make the call."

Thirty minutes later they were all sitting at the round oak table in the kitchen eating pizza and drinking root beer. Half of the pizza was pepperoni and half was cheese, and Tommy, who never wanted anything but plain cheese, watched Cade eat a pepperoni slice and decided he wanted one, too. Rachel nearly fell out of her chair when Tommy inhaled the slice and wanted more.

Cade watched Tommy eat a second pepperoni slice, holding the wedge with both hands, his eyes big and bright, but his expression was dreamy and unfocused, and he seemed far away.

He was a sweet kid, Cade thought, a quiet little boy who lived in his own world, but that didn't bother him. Growing up, Cade had been fairly disconnected from the world, too, and sometimes it was better to be distant and dreamy than aware of all the chaos and pain.

So far Rachel hadn't said anything about Tommy's father, and frankly, Cade didn't want to know much, having already formed an opinion of Tommy's father and it wasn't flattering. Any man who would walk away from his own child was an A-hole and a loser, and both Rachel and Tommy deserved better.

Suddenly Tommy looked up at Cade and smiled. "Pizza," Tommy said, tomato sauce smudging his mouth as he grinned broadly.

"It's good, isn't it?" Cade answered, smiling back at the boy, aware that this was the first time Tommy had ever spoken directly to him.

Tommy continued to grin and eat, watching Cade's face as he chewed, and something shifted and ached in Cade's chest.

It was ironic, but with his dark hair and big blue eyes, Tommy looked an awful lot like Cade and could easily pass for his son, just as Cade had looked like his father, rodeo cowboy legend Jack King, who'd died at twenty-seven when his horse had rolled on him during the saddle bronc competition. It was a freak accident—and rare—as most fatalities in the sport came from bull riding, and even then there had only been three in the PRCA since 2000—but it made big news.

Cade wasn't much older than Tommy when his dad died, just five, but he remembered the funeral and all the cowboys who attended, and how so many of them clapped him on the shoulder, or patted his head, and told him one day he'd be a great cowboy, too, just like his dad.

Funny. Cade rarely thought about his dad, despite becoming a rodeo champion in his own right, but remembering his childhood never felt good and he'd learned to get through life by focusing on the next event, the next road trip and the next prize to be won.

"Done," Tommy said, pointing to the hall. "Go. LEGOs."

"You had enough to eat?" Rachel asked, leaning across the table to wipe his mouth off.

Tommy nodded so Rachel excused him, and Cade watched Rachel watch her son dash down the hall and he felt his chest grow tight again. She loved her son so much, and her love was so pure and so unconditional that it moved him deeply. She was so different from his mother, who wasn't a maternal woman...

Abruptly he stood and gathered the plates and cups and carried everything to the sink, turning the faucet on to rinse the plates clean.

"Leave it," Rachel said from behind him. "I'll do it later."

"I'm here. Let me help."

"You've helped so much already today, Cade. You saved me."

"I did nothing—"

"Nothing? You were an answer to my prayer! If it weren't

for you, Mia wouldn't have had a cake, and what's a wedding without a cake?"

"Not much of a wedding," he agreed, turning off the water to smile at her, his expression warm. "But it was my pleasure to drive you there, and attend the reception with you. You looked so happy…it made me happy to see you smile and laugh with your friends. I have a feeling you don't get to see your girlfriends as much as you used to."

Her mouth curved and yet he saw a shadow in her eyes. "No, but someday they'll be moms and we'll have more in common again." And then just like that the shadow was gone and she was sitting forward in her seat, smiling mischievously at him. "And you, Cade King, were quite popular at the reception. Seems like you knew everybody. There was a line of folks waiting to talk to you all afternoon. I swear you were more popular than the bride and groom."

"I sure hope not, considering I wasn't invited."

Rachel laughed. "You might not have been invited, but Mia was thrilled you were there. She'll be telling everybody for the next year that a celebrity attended her wedding."

Cade grew warm, uncomfortable with talk like that. "I'm not a celebrity," he growled. "And I was there as your wheels. Your assistant. Your driver."

Her lips pursed and she arched a dark eyebrow. "My chauffeur?"

"Exactly."

She gave her head a faint shake, even as her gaze searched his. "You really didn't mind racing around, wrestling with my cake, dealing with my car?"

"Best day I've had in years."

"Stop it."

He drew an *X* on his chest. "Cross my heart, Rachel James."

Her lower lip quivered before she bit down hard into it. "You're killing me."

"Why?"

"You're too good with lines."

"They're not lines, Rache," he said earnestly, wishing he could reach for her, touch her, take her into his arms. "I mean everything I say. I loved being with you today. It felt good. Right—"

"So, how long do you think it'll be until my car will be ready?" she asked, jumping to her feet, reaching for the bottle of root beer and screwing the cap on. She walked quickly to the refrigerator and put the root beer away, but the tumble of dark hair around her face only highlighted how pale she'd gotten.

Cade silently kicked himself, wishing he could take the words back. What was the matter with him? Why make her uncomfortable? "At least two or three days," he said. "Maybe more, depending on how hard it is to find the parts and complete the labor. But Phil will call you in the morning once he's been able to assess things better."

"Will it be expensive?" she asked, crossing her arms over her chest.

Cade hesitated. "Probably."

"How expensive?"

"Could be anywhere from six hundred to nine hundred dollars."

"*Nine* hundred?"

"Provided you don't need a new engine."

Panic flared in her eyes. "Seriously?"

Cade jutted his jaw, feeling like hell. "Not what you want to hear, huh?"

"No. Accountants might be busy this time of year, but not wedding-cake folks. We slow after Valentine's Day and, yes, it'll pick up late April, but…" Her voice trailed off and then she shrugged and forced a smile. "I'm going to go check on Tommy."

Down the hall in Tommy's room, Rachel leaned against the doorway watching him line up his miniature LEGO figurines. Pirates and ninjas and little Harry Potters. She loved watching him play and how engrossed he became in his activity. And he'd always loved his room. From the time he was a toddler, it'd been his sanctuary. He'd miss this room, and so would she.

She was still watching Tommy when Cade came to find her a few minutes later. "Everything okay?" he asked.

Her skin prickled with awareness as he came up behind her. She might not want to be attracted to Cade anymore, but her body certainly knew he was there. "Yes," she said, flashing him a quick smile. "Just thinking. I've lived in this house ever since Tommy was born."

"There must be a lot of good memories here."

"Hundreds," Rachel agreed, thinking of the green-and-white nursery she'd decorated for Tommy and the cheerful Beatrix Potter quilt Grandma had sewn for his crib before making a matching quilt to hang on the wall.

"What's your new place like?" Cade asked.

"Nice," she said quickly, maybe too quickly, because she saw the lift of Cade's eyebrows. "Of course it'll need a little TLC. Every place does. But it'll be good once we're all settled."

"You're taking the furniture?"

Rachel glanced past him, back down the hall, toward the kitchen with its solid, scratched oak table, but it was a table she loved more than anything, and then to the dining room and living room beyond.

"As much as I can," she answered, her fingers curling into a fist that she pressed against her ribs. She wouldn't be taking the kitchen table with her. She couldn't. It wouldn't fit through the narrow apartment doorways. And yet that table represented her grandmother more than anything else in this place. Grandma Sally sat there every morning with her coffee and every night at dinner with her iced tea. And it was home. And maybe it was silly, because it was just a piece of furniture, but it made her feel loved. "It's an apartment, not a house," she added, huskily, "so not everything will fit."

If Cade heard the break in her voice he gave no indication. "When do you move?"

"The new people are moving in on the sixteenth, but I have to be out by the fourteenth so they can clean on the fifteenth—"

"You're moving on Valentine's Day?"

She rolled her eyes. "Valentine's Day isn't a big deal to me, and Tommy doesn't care, so it's not something we focus on around here."

"Can I help you with the move?"

"I've already got that handled." She glanced around Tommy's room, which would be the last room packed since he didn't like his things disturbed. She needed to go through his toys, too, and donate the things he'd outgrown or didn't play with, but she was so sentimental. Many of the toys symbolized the early years. The years when she hadn't known what was wrong with Tommy, only that something was wrong with Tommy, even though doctors just told her not to worry so much, that boys were often developmentally delayed, that many little boys struggled with speech…

But she'd known. She'd known that something wasn't right when a baby wouldn't look at his mother. She'd known in her heart that it wasn't supposed to be like this…her baby should smile…look into her eyes…. Tommy did neither.

Cade frowned. "Won't that be expensive?"

"I'm doing it as a barter. A wedding cake in exchange for two guys and a truck for three hours."

"That's smart."

"Mmm," she agreed, unwilling to let Cade know how hard it'd been to find someone who would barter the move. Rachel had never had a lot of money, and paying for Tommy's specialists and therapists was a constant strain, but it was worth it. Already the weekly speech and occupational-therapy sessions had made a difference.

"Where is his dad, Rachel?" Cade asked quietly.

Rachel glanced quickly at Tommy before moving away from his door and walking back to the kitchen. "Calgary," she said, picking up the plates Cade had rinsed and adding them to the dishwasher.

Cade drew out a chair at the table and sat down. "He's Canadian?"

"No. David's from Dallas. I met him at a bar in Fort Worth one night when I was out with Mia and some of the other girls." She added the root-beer glasses to the top rack, closed the dishwasher door and faced Cade. "From far away David looks like you—tall, dark, handsome. But he wasn't you." She grimaced and shrugged. "Definitely wasn't you, and we only went out a couple times, but I somehow still managed to get pregnant."

"And David doesn't want to be part of Tommy's life?"

"He gave me money for an abortion before leaving town." She lifted her chin, looked Cade square in the eye. "I didn't love David. He was a rebound thing, but there was no way I could get rid of the baby. So I took the seven hundred and fifty dollars he gave me and opened a savings account for Tommy's college education. And maybe Tommy won't go to college, but he's going to have an amazing life. I've given up on a lot of dreams these past few years, but I'm not giving up that one."

Chapter Five

Before Cade could think of an answer, Tommy walked into the kitchen with the television remote.

"Show," Tommy said, holding out the remote to Cade.

Cade glanced at Rachel. "Can I turn on the TV for him?" he asked, rising.

Rachel sighed and rubbed at her forehead. "Yes, but he won't be happy. He wants a particular program—"

"Show," Tommy interrupted, impatiently pushing the remote into Cade's hand before walking out. He glanced over his shoulder at Cade and gestured for him to follow. "Scooby."

Cade followed him to the living room and hit Power on the remote. It took a moment before the old TV flickered on.

"Scooby," Tommy repeated, looking expectantly at Cade.

"Scooby-Doo?" Cade answered. "You like that show? I do, too."

Tommy flinched, facial muscles twitching before he nodded and smiled, a jerky little smile. "Scooby. Shaaag... Shaaggy."

"Scooby and Shaggy are my favorites."

Tommy's mouth twisted again but this time no sound came out and he simply smiled.

"Hey, Rache, what channel is your Cartoon Network?" Cade called to her, thinking she was still in the kitchen.

"We don't get cable anymore," she said quietly from right behind him. "Just the regular free stuff. But he doesn't understand. We won't have cable until we move."

"Don't you have a DVD he could watch?"

She sighed. "It broke last month."

"Scooby," Tommy insisted.

Rachel raised her voice. "Tommy, we can't watch Scooby-Doo right now, but I'll see what else is on," she said cheerfully but firmly. "Maybe we can find a kids' show on another channel."

The boy's mouth worked, his features tightening and grimacing. "Scoob. Mama."

"We'll find another show you can watch, Tommy," Rachel repeated, even more firmly. "I'm sure there is something fun on—"

"Scooob, Mama. Tommmy…good boy."

"We can't watch Scooby, Tommy—"

Tommy let out one of his piercing wails and Cade suddenly couldn't breathe, his chest on fire. "You can get DVD players cheap now, Rachel," Cade said shortly, angry, so angry, and not even knowing why.

"Not cheap enough," she answered, raising her voice even louder to be heard over Tommy's wailing.

Cade's gut hurt. His emotions were so damn raw. "I've seen them for sixty-five bucks—"

"And that sixty-five bucks will pay for ten hours of child care or buy groceries or pay for a half hour of speech therapy," she snapped, facing him. Color flooded her cheeks, making her gray eyes luminous. "So I have to make choices, and they need to be good choices, and unfortunately buying a cheap DVD player so Tommy can watch Scooby-Doo isn't one of them!"

Cade's chest grew tighter and he drew a short, rough breath, temper simmering. "It's that bad around here?"

"I wouldn't call it bad. I'd call it tight. But it's always been tight. And maybe it's a struggle but it's a good struggle, because I'm making it…I'm doing it. I'm taking care of my boy and I don't need David or you or any other man to waltz into my life like you're some fairy godfather and make things better."

"I'm not interested in being a fairy godfather. I just want to get you a DVD player. Please."

"That's not necessary. But thank you."

Tommy moved behind Rachel, and began bumping his face repeatedly into her hip. "Scoob. Show."

"Rachel, it's sixty-five dollars. And it'd make him happy."

Her chin lifted even as she put a hand behind her to stop Tommy from pushing against her. "A lot of things would make us happy—a new car and hot-fudge sundaes and a trip to Disneyland, but that doesn't mean we're going to get them—" she held up a hand to stop him when he would have interrupted "—and I'm okay with that. Those are luxuries. I—we—don't need luxuries. What we need is speech therapy and physical therapy and occupational therapy and doctors and teachers, and those all cost money. A lot of money." She swallowed hard, and her chin jerked even higher. "But I'm doing it…I'm giving him every important thing I can."

Cade clamped his jaw tight, his narrowed gaze taking in her compressed lips and fierce expression. He'd forgotten how stubborn she was. And strong. And proud. "It's a housewarming present for your new apartment," he said.

"Kind of you, but not necessary."

"It's not for you, it's for Tommy."

"He respectfully declines."

"You can't reject gifts I give to him."

"Oh, yes, I can. I'm his mother."

"Why are you doing this?"

"Why are you?"

"Because I care about you, Rachel."

Her hands balled into fists. For a moment she said nothing, her eyes sparkling with tears she wouldn't cry. "Too little, too late," she choked.

She'd said it quietly, but he'd heard, just as she'd meant for him to hear. And even though Cade knew she was right, it still felt as if she'd shoved a kitchen knife between his ribs.

"Sounds like my cue to leave," he said.

"That's probably a good idea."

AN HOUR LATER, ARRIVING home at his ranch, Cade headed to the barn and checked on his horses before heading to the house where his yellow lab, Lacey, was curled up in the family room in her makeshift nursery with her litter of pups. The puppies were six weeks now and soon they'd be heading to new homes.

Cade sat on the ground next to Lacey and scratched behind her ears, crooning compliments as he gave her some love. "You're a good momma, Lacey girl. So patient with all these demanding little guys crawling all over you."

Lacey put her head on his thigh and thumped her tail.

"Don't you worry," he said, rubbing behind the other ear before giving her chin a scratch, "you'll be sleeping upstairs again soon. You won't be stuck down here in the family room forever."

He gave her another rub and scratch before rising, and checked over the six blond puppies, who were pretty damn irresistible, then dimmed the lights and headed upstairs for the night.

In his master bath, Cade took a shower and changed into baggy flannel pajama pants and a soft, stretched-out T-shirt before climbing into bed. But once in bed he couldn't sleep. He pounded his pillows repeatedly trying to get comfortable, but sleep wouldn't come. Every time he closed his eyes, he saw Rachel's face, and he could see the creases in her forehead and the worry darken her eyes. Even in the dark of his room he could see how she stood, arms tightly crossed over her chest, her full soft mouth pulled into a thin line, as if holding all of her anxiety and pain in.

She didn't want his help, but she needed help. And no, not a fairy godfather kind of help—he shuddered in bed, thinking the very idea was horrible—but support. Love. Someone she could lean on. Someone who could be another pair of hands as well as ears and eyes and everything else it took to raise a child. Because children were work and expensive, and Tommy was no different.

Unwittingly, Cade flashed back to when he was a boy and living with his mom, a woman completely different from Rachel, a woman who wasn't maternal or patient. His mom was a woman who needed a man, not a child, and she hadn't enjoyed spending time with him, preferring to hang out in honky-tonk bars, taverns and pool halls, always looking out for the next guy to sweep her off her feet and make her problems go away. Or at the very least, take her to bed and give her a place to stay for a week or two.

Child-protection services had removed Cade from Mama's care when he was seven, placing him in foster care. She got him back six months later, but lost him less than a year after that. Cade was reunited with her one week before his ninth birthday and they had ten great months together before everything started falling apart again, and by the time he was ten, he was back in foster care. Cade spent sixth grade counting the days down until his mom claimed him, and then seventh grade, and was still waiting in eighth when it dawned on him that maybe this time she wasn't coming back.

He didn't give up hope, though. He couldn't. Foster care wasn't much better than living with an alcoholic mother, and he'd rather have his mother—even if she did stay out all night—than be thrust into a house with a bunch of strangers.

He was still waiting for her at fifteen when he "borrowed" a car and went to find her, finally tracking her down in Willow Park where she was shacked up with some guy in a trailer on a crappy piece of land. She'd been surprised to see him, crying and hugging him, said he was the spitting image of his father but even handsomer, then offered him a drink—rum and Coke, her favorite. He took it. And then another, and another. But when her boyfriend came home late that afternoon he wasn't pleased to see Cade and things got heated and Cade got tossed.

Cade left his foster family's car somewhere they could find it, and then he took off, hitchhiking out of Parker County and going as far as the truckers would take him.

Cade ended up in Wyoming, got a job at the Frank B. Douglas Ranch, outside Cheyenne, working for peanuts and a place to stay, but he liked working with horses, wasn't intimidated by the cows or bulls. It turned out he had a knack for riding and roping and, after being encouraged by Mr. Douglas himself, entered his first junior rodeo at seventeen in Casper. Cade didn't win anything but did well enough that he entered three more that summer. By the end of the summer he was placing and taking home prize money. By eighteen he was winning consistently. At nineteen he joined the PRCA and started competing in open events, with Douglas Ranch as his first sponsor.

Cade never knew until later that Frank Douglas Sr. had once competed on the circuit himself and had known Cade's father—not well, but well enough to take an interest in Cade King. And Cade had never forgotten that it wasn't blood that got him through, it was the time and patience of a stranger. Cade had often wondered what he would have become if Frank hadn't allowed Cade, just a teenage runaway, to crash for a night or two while he figured out what he was going to do.

Giving up on sleep, Cade left his bed and headed back downstairs to his office and his desktop computer. Flipping on the light, he sat down in front of the screen and clicked on the internet, and then typed in *autism,* hit Enter and began to read.

RACHEL WOKE UP SUNDAY morning tense, jittery and edgy, and her mood just worsened throughout the day. For some reason she kept expecting Cade to call or drop by. She didn't know why—she certainly didn't want him to come by—but he'd stirred something up inside of her, and she was mad this morning, really mad, and she wanted him to know it. She wanted him to feel her wrath and her disappointment, as well as her disgust.

Who did he think he was, waltzing back into her life five-plus years later, acting as if he had a right to be in her life?

He had no rights when it came to her or Sally or the past. He'd known from the moment he met her how she felt about drinking, having lost her parents at thirteen when a drunk driver slammed into their car, killing them instantly.

Rachel had never been okay with alcohol, much less drinking and driving. Or drinking and riding. Or drinking and fighting. And Cade knew it. But that didn't stop him from eventually wanting liquor, needing liquor, more than he wanted her, and so when she put her foot down, telling him to get help or risk losing her, he chose to walk away.

No, correction—*run* away. Because that's exactly what he'd done. Because it sure was easier to leave her than try to change.

For over five years she'd heard nothing from him. Not a word. But now he was back, and because he'd gone to some

AA meetings and apologized for being a jerk, he thought he could give her advice and tell her what to do…

Ha! And she was going to tell him that, too.

But Cade didn't call on Sunday. He didn't call Monday, either. She did hear from the mechanic, though, and the tow-truck driver was right. Her blown head gasket had caused her Jeep to overheat, which had put an ugly crack in the engine, and she needed a new engine.

Before Rachel could truly panic, Phil, the mechanic, said he had an engine that might work for her. It wasn't a new engine, but it was in a lot better shape than the one he'd just pulled out of her Jeep, and she could have it if she wanted it, provided she'd pay for the labor to get it installed.

Rachel felt a massive wave of relief, followed by an uncomfortable prick of suspicion. "Did Cade tell you to do this?"

"What's that, ma'am?"

"Did Cade King tell you to do this?"

"Fix your car, ma'am?"

Rachel sighed, knowing she was sounding a bit crazy, and maybe that's because she was feeling crazy. "Never mind. It's great, and I appreciate you helping me out like this. When do you think it'll be done?"

"I'm shooting for tomorrow afternoon, but it might be Wednesday morning. I'll call you as soon as it's ready."

"Thank you."

Hanging up, she stared at the phone for a long moment before summoning her courage and dialing Cade's number. But he didn't answer and her call went to voice mail, so Rachel left him a brief message. "No need to call me back. Just wanted you to know that my car will be ready tomorrow afternoon or Wednesday morning. If you can still give me a ride to the garage, that would be great. Thanks." And then she hung up, put her phone down on the counter and forced herself to resume packing as if nothing had happened.

As if calling Cade King was routine and thinking of him didn't still hurt. And remembering the way he left her didn't make her angry and furious, and crazy as hell.

But she didn't like feeling this way. She didn't like the intense emotions churning inside her, aware that being angry was just as bad as being helpless, and neither accomplished anything. Angry didn't change the fact she'd gotten pregnant, and angry didn't save Grandma. No, angry just made her feel small and mean and that was no way to live. Since Grandma's death, Rachel had dedicated herself to making her life—and Tommy's life—as warm and wonderful as possible. Because life, even if hard, even if painful, could still shimmer and shine and be full of beauty, love and good things.

At one on Tuesday, Phil called from his Weatherford garage to say her Jeep would be ready by two. Rachel phoned Cade immediately, and he answered immediately, too, as if expecting her call. Cade told her he was wrapping up a meeting with Jeffrey Farms and could pick her up within the hour, if that worked for her. She told him it would, and then she got Tommy dressed—never easy when he didn't want to put on real clothes, far preferring to be naked, which didn't go over big when they were in public places—and then she changed into a soft pair of Wrangler jeans and a cream peasant-style blouse with blue embroidery. She fluffed her dark hair and swirled some mascara onto her lashes, before slicking pink gloss onto her lips.

Rachel didn't know why she was making an effort to look nice. Did she hope he'd want her back? That he'd realize he'd made a massive mistake and that she was everything—and more—than she'd been before?

Just then Tommy screamed from his room. She knew

the scream. It wasn't a panic scream, but one of frustration. He'd probably gotten impatient with something and then thrown it, or hit it, and broken it. It's how they'd lost the DVD player. It's how so many of his toys ended up in the garbage.

She was still calming Tommy down, consoling him over shattering his Little Critter car, when the doorbell rang. She gulped a panicked breath. Cade had arrived.

Chapter Six

The car wasn't ready.

Reaching Weatherford, they arrived at the garage, only to discover that although the new engine was in, the car still wasn't running correctly. Apparently there was an issue with the alternator.

Rachel stood outside the garage, looking at her gray Jeep where it was sitting in the pit with its hood propped open, listening to Phil's explanation. He earnestly explained in great detail what alternators did, and why she needed a new one, and how horrible he felt about hitting her with this now on top of the new engine. The good news was that he should have it done by five if she could give him another couple hours.

She nodded when it seemed appropriate, letting his words stream over her while she tried not to think of what her bank account would look like by the time she finally got her car back. Thank goodness she'd already put her first month's rent down on the apartment—along with the last—or she wouldn't have a place to go ten days from now.

"So that gives us two, two and a half hours," Cade said, looking at Rachel and then at Tommy, who was hanging on to Rachel and her coat as if they were a piece of playground equipment. "Do you have errands you need to run?"

Rachel wouldn't let herself think of all the things she wanted to buy...groceries, that DVD player, a new pair of shoes for Tommy…and shook her head. "Nope. We're in good shape."

"Is there anything you want to do?"

She thought of her small house and the things still to be packed, but shook her head again. "No."

"I have an idea, then," Cade said. "I didn't know if Tommy liked dogs, or was scared of them…?"

"He likes them," she said drily, knowing that once he found a dog, he was like flypaper. It was almost impossible to peel him off. "A lot."

"Lacey, my lab, had puppies six weeks ago, and I thought I'd take you to the ranch so Tommy could see them. They're cute as heck and the ranch isn't far. Twenty minutes away."

Rachel knew there were reasons they shouldn't go, but Tommy would love to see the puppies. The pet store in Mineral Wells was his favorite place to go and he couldn't handle the puppies there but he spent hours crouched in front of their cages looking at them. "He'd love it. He's never held a puppy before but he loves them. Half of his picture books are about dogs."

They'd been walking to the truck as they talked, and she watched now as Cade lifted Tommy into the back and secured him into his booster seat. Cade did it smoothly, easily, as if he'd been lifting children into car seats his entire life. And she told herself not to be impressed—if he could bridle a horse and rope a calf and wrestle a steer, he could certainly buckle a four-year-old into a booster seat—but Tommy didn't like to be touched. He didn't want help. But for whatever reason, he allowed Cade to touch him. He wanted Cade to help him. Interesting.

Climbing into the front passenger seat, Rachel buckled her own seat belt and glanced at Cade as he opened the driver-side door and slid behind the steering wheel, wondering what it was about Cade that put Tommy at ease, because normally Tommy didn't like men or big people.

He preferred older women…gentle women, women like Grandma or Mrs. Munoz, and Cade was most definitely not like either of them.

But then, Cade was calm, and he had a different energy—relaxed, laid-back—and animals responded to it, particularly young animals and high-strung horses. She wouldn't go so far as to call him a horse whisperer, but often all he had to do was touch an animal for it to settle down, relax. Maybe he had the same effect on Tommy.

She looked over her shoulder at Tommy in his car seat. He was crooning to himself and looking out the window, as happy as could be. He hated the car, yet he liked Cade's truck.

Of course her boy would love Cade. She'd once loved him, too.

A lump filled her throat and, swallowing hard, she looked out the window, hands balling in her lap.

But she couldn't go there. Wouldn't go there. Life was hard enough without giving in to memories and wishful thinking. Better to remain focused and disciplined. Better to think about what was, rather than what could have been. Far fewer expectations that way. Less opportunity for disappointment and pain. And she was a realist now. Life and experience had made sure of that. She didn't dream dreams for herself anymore. Her dreams were for Tommy. It was Tommy who mattered now.

"I haven't had a drink in over two years, Rachel," Cade said, his deep voice breaking the silence.

Rachel stiffened, surprised, and more than a little uncomfortable, feeling as if he'd somehow peeked into her mind and seen what she was thinking.

"I'm done with drinking. It might be okay for some people, but it's not a good thing for me." He looked at her, his blue gaze steady, piercing. "It never was a good thing for me."

She opened her mouth, then closed it, not knowing what

to say. What did he want her to say? *Great, Cade, I'm proud of you.*

"You were right," he added, his voice a little deeper, a little rougher. "But you know that. I just want you to know that you were always right. You did the correct thing, too, telling me to sober up. I'm glad you were strong enough to do it. And I'm also glad you weren't there to see me hit rock bottom…it got pretty ugly before I figured out the drinking wasn't working."

"So what was your lightbulb moment? What sobered you up?"

He hesitated so long that she wasn't sure he was going to answer, and then he said bluntly, "I drove my truck into a tree, going eighty miles an hour."

She shot him a swift glance. "Did you miss a bend in the road?"

A small muscle popped in his jaw. "No. Meant to do it." His right hand tightened on the steering wheel. "I was racing my demons that night and they won."

"Cade," she whispered, chest aching, eyes burning. Because as mad as she was at Cade, the idea of a world without Cade didn't make sense to her. A world without Cade was no world at all.

Over the years, yes, part of her had hated him. But a bigger part of her had loved him, and maybe it was crazy, but just loving him a little bit from afar had kept her going when nothing else did. And even though she couldn't talk about him with Mia or any of her other friends, she was secretly glad he'd done well on the circuit. She was happy when he climbed in the standings and proud when he won. Maybe they couldn't be together but she wanted good things for him. No, she wanted great things for him. Not because she was selfless and all altruistic, but because she'd loved him that much. It was impossible to love someone that much without wanting what was best for them, and that's all there was to it.

"Good thing you didn't die," she said tartly, lifting her chin and giving Cade a fierce look. "Because then I couldn't have given you a piece of my mind, Cade King, and I promise you, when we don't have little ears listening, I'm going to tell you exactly what I think about you and your drinking and your demons."

Cade's gaze locked with hers for a second before he focused on the road, but she saw the corners of his mouth curl and creases fan from the edges of his eyes. "You do that, darlin'," he drawled. "You give me that piece of your mind. And don't hold anything back, either, because Lord knows, I have it coming."

And just like that, a little crack formed in the ice coating her insides and she had to draw a very careful breath to keep the crack from growing any bigger.

She could like Cade and want the best for him, but she couldn't get carried away. She knew who Cade was and what he was, and he might be gorgeous and good with animals and children, but he wasn't good for her. He wasn't. And she had to remember that. Had to remember what loving Cade had done to her.

Ten minutes later, Cade slowed before a large gate, and the automatic gate slowly swung open, and then they were driving across the cattle guard, the big black truck rattling as they crossed the bars. But the ranch house was another five minutes off the road, and Rachel watched scenery, studying the fenced pastures, and the clusters of oak trees and elm trees, and the gleam of a distant pond or lake. She and Cade used to go look at ranches when they were together, pretending they had the money to buy something, and they'd talk about what they liked about a particular piece of property, and what was lacking…

"It's called Sweetwater," Cade said, gently braking and veering right, turning into a large circular driveway that connected a cluster of ranch buildings, "for the two streams and lake on the property." And then he was parking in front of a house made from Texas limestone, the simple house fronted by a deep veranda. Six rough-hewn pillars supported the porch, drawing the eye upward to the three windows jutting out of the steeply pitched roof. The bedrooms, Rachel guessed, glancing up.

"Home," Cade said, turning the engine off.

Just then Lacey came bounding from around the corner, thrilled to see Cade, and Tommy shrieked in the backseat, arms outstretched. "Dog!"

Cade laughed and looked at Rachel. "He really does like dogs."

"Loves them."

"Wait until he sees the puppies."

IT WAS A DAY SHE'D NEVER forget, Rachel thought, watching Tommy sit in the middle of the family room, surrounded by gorgeous, fluffy golden puppies that wanted nothing more than to crawl over him, and lick him, and burrow into his hands. And Tommy—bless him, her beautiful boy—was so gentle and his expression was so full of joy, that it made her heart ache, and she had to fight tears to see a child that people didn't understand and want to understand just love and be loved.

And maybe they were only puppies but still, love was love, and Tommy was in heaven. He was. Now and then he'd let out a little yelp, inarticulate with joy, and Lacey would go to him and give his face a lick, as if he was one of her pups, too. Rachel suddenly turned away as Tommy nuzzled Lacey back, kissing her soft muzzle as if that were the most natural thing in the world for him to do.

She walked to the window and stared out, a hand pressed to her mouth, fighting tears, fighting joy, fighting to maintain control because life wasn't easy for them, and few things were simple for Tommy. But this was, and she was grateful. Grateful that for a couple hours her son could just be, and be happy, and good…not good as in well behaved, but good as in peaceful. Good as in complete and perfect just the way he was made.

"You okay?" It was Cade, and she'd heard his boots as he'd come up behind her but she couldn't totally pull herself together in time.

Rachel nodded, wiping away tears, keeping her back to him.

"What's wrong?"

She shook her head.

"But you're crying."

"He kissed Lacey," she whispered, her voice cracking.

"Is that bad?"

She shook her head, wiping tears that suddenly wouldn't stop. "No. It's good. Sweet." She gulped a breath and struggled to smile through her tears. "It's just that…he doesn't kiss me."

Cade would never forget that moment. Never. It would be burned into his mind for the rest of his life.

Her face. Those gray eyes, filled with tears and shimmering like silver. Her lips trembling, struggling to smile. And those words. Just four little words.

He doesn't kiss me.

Cade reeled inwardly, sucker punched, as it hit him harder than ever before just what his girl had been going through.

Bravely. Uncomplainingly.

If it'd be okay for a man to cry, he would have cried right then and there because his heart was breaking for Rachel, and for the life she'd lived while he'd been riding bulls and broncs and trying to figure out which end was up and learning how to forgive himself, never mind like himself.

But he'd gotten to the other side of some dark, scary stuff and he was still here, and he was stronger for it. And God help him, but his scars and toughness had to count for something. His scars and banged-up heart still had to be good for something.

They had to be.

"You've raised a beautiful boy, Rachel. You have. You should be proud of yourself."

And then she did the unthinkable. She turned into his arms and leaned against him, her wet face pressed to his chest, and cried. *Cried.* Real tears, hard tears, hot tears, and it hurt to know his lovely Rachel had so much pain inside, but he wasn't going anywhere ever again. She might not know it yet, and she might never believe it, but Cade was in it for the long haul this time. She was his world and his future and his heart. And it might take him years to win her back, but he would.

His big hand settled on the back of her head, and gently, carefully, he stroked her hair, his palm smoothing the straight, silky strands. While he hated that she was crying as if her heart was breaking, he was glad he could hold her, and glad he could finally be there for her, because late was still better than never.

It was hard pulling Tommy away from Lacey and her puppies but Cade finally managed to get Tommy out of the house and into his booster seat in the truck, after explaining to him that the puppies were just little tiny babies and they were hungry and needed to eat and sleep.

Tommy had made a little crooning sound, and then he leaned over and kissed each puppy somewhere on the head or back or butt—as he did with the last one who was wiggling toward Lacey for dinner—and waved goodbye. Now they were all having dinner at Cade's favorite café in Weatherford.

Rachel ordered chicken nuggets for Tommy—one of the few foods he'd eat—and a grilled-cheese sandwich and tomato soup for herself. And Cade sat in the booth, dipping his French dip into the au jus, feeling so many different things that he didn't know how he kept it all in.

This is what it'd be like, he thought, watching Rachel pop chicken bites into Tommy's mouth as Tommy stared off in space, a dreamy expression on his face.

This is what it'd be like if they were a family...if they were his family. And the thought wrenched something deep inside his chest.

It'd been a long time since he'd had a family. He'd hungered to be part of one since he was a little boy, and then when he understood at fifteen it wasn't going to happen, he set out on his own, trying to forget who he was and where he'd come from. It'd been eighteen years since he'd hitchhiked out of Texas, but he'd never forgotten that first week on the road—the nights at truck stops, the mornings and afternoons standing alongside the highway with his thumb out, the moments he had to duck or run when he saw a highway-patrol car, certain the police were coming after him.

He'd always remember the cities he passed through, too—Abilene, Lubbock, Amarillo, Albuquerque, Santa Fe, Pueblo, Colorado Springs, Denver, Fort Collins, Cheyenne—before finally meeting Jasper Smythe, the ranch foreman for the Douglas Ranch, who let the exhausted teenager crash for a night in the bunkhouse, and then for another night, before introducing him to the Douglas family, who took a chance on him and gave him his first real job.

Sometimes all people needed was a chance.

Cade looked from Tommy's dreamy expression to Rachel's

tense one, aware that she was doing her best to keep him at arm's length, but Cade wasn't daunted. All he needed was a chance. And Rachel, whether she knew it or not, was giving him that chance right now, and this time there was no way he was going to blow it.

RACHEL'S PHONE RANG WHILE Tommy was carefully eating the frosting off his slice of chocolate cake. He didn't like cake, but loved frosting, and she'd been trying not to smile at how finicky he was with every cake crumb.

"Phil," she said to Cade, picking up her phone to take the call.

Cade reached for his wallet. "Tell him we're on the way."

But answering, Phil apologized and told her that despite his best effort, he wasn't going to be able to finish her car tonight. He was really sorry and knew it was an inconvenience, but it was late and his daughter had a basketball game and he couldn't miss it.

Rachel told him she understood and that it wasn't a problem, but hanging up, her stomach churned with anxiety and frustration. She wanted her car back. She wanted her life back. She wanted to feel as though she had some control again.

"Not good news," Cade said, catching sight of her face.

"No." She sighed. "Looks like you'll have to play chauffeur another day longer."

"What happened?"

"I don't know. Everything's back together but something's still not working. The car's not idling right or it dies while idling, despite replacing the alternator, and Phil doesn't have any more time to figure it out tonight—"

"Yes, he does," Cade interrupted, reaching for his phone. "He's not going home and leaving you without your car for another day. That's ridiculous. I'm going to tell him to suck it up and work late—"

"Don't." She stretched a hand across the table, placing her fingers over his, stopping him from dialing Phil's number. "His daughter has a basketball game. He needs to be there."

"No—"

"Yes," she said firmly. "He does. Trust me. He does. I can make it another day without a car."

Cade didn't answer. He was looking at her hand where it rested on his, and she glanced down, seeing what he saw... her fingers on his, her skin pale against his bronze skin, and her skin tingled, not just where they touched, but everywhere.

Suddenly too warm, Rachel pulled her hand away and busied herself gathering coats and her purse. "Ready?" she asked, feeling breathless.

"Yep." Cade slid out of the booth.

Rachel tried to get Tommy into his coat, but he was facing Cade, his arms out to him. "Dog?" he said hopefully.

"No, honey," Rachel answered, tugging Tommy toward her, trying to slip his arm into one sleeve. "Not tonight. Maybe another time."

"Dog." Tommy pulled his arm out of the coat and leaned past Rachel to look up at Cade. His hands made circles in the air. "Pup...pup...puppies. Cade h-h-house."

"No, Tommy," she said, struggling to be patient, but it was hard at the end of the day. Her patience tended to wear thin about now. "Not tonight. It's time to go home."

He wailed. "Mama!"

"And Mama said no, Tommy." She wrestled his right arm into his coat and then the left and zipped it quickly before he could stop her.

"Puppies. Dog. Cade house. Tommy good boy. Tommy go—"

She exhaled hard, exhausted, frustrated. *"No."*

"Why not?" Cade asked quietly.

Rachel stared up at him, startled, before glancing out the café windows at the dark sky. "It's…getting late."

"It's just a little after six now."

"But if we go back, it'll be almost impossible getting him out later. You remember how difficult it was dragging him away from Lacey and her puppies in the first place."

He shrugged. "So stay the night."

"What?"

He shrugged again, even more casually than before. "Stay the night, and I'll take you to Phil's garage to get your car in the morning as soon as it's done."

"We can't," she spluttered.

"Why not?"

Rachel scrambled to think of a good, practical reason, one he couldn't argue with and, sadly, she couldn't think of a single one. There was no cat or dog waiting to be fed. There was no family member waiting, or someone who would disapprove. There was nothing urgent to be done but pack, and she still had a week before they had to move.

Tommy had been following the conversation and he grabbed his mother's sleeve. "Dog?" he asked hopefully, his blue eyes light, sparkling, and suddenly he looked like the little boy she'd always imagined he'd be…present and focused and beautifully alive.

"You and Tommy could share a room, or you could both have your own rooms. Either way, you'd have total privacy, Rache," Cade said. "And then as soon as Phil calls to say your car is ready, I'll drive you straight to the garage."

Rachel exhaled and looked down into Tommy's face. His blue eyes shone with eagerness, his gaze focused on her face, waiting for her response. He literally glowed right now with life. This was one of those moments, she thought, that the therapists had said were significant because they helped his brain rewire, allowing him to make new connections, connections that would allow him to communicate better with the world.

Ironic, she thought, lightly touching his cheek, that he came to life around Cade?

Or not.

Grandma had always said Cade would do great things one day. Maybe Grandma was right.

"Okay," she murmured, glancing up at Cade. "Just be prepared for Tommy to change his mind and have a total meltdown. It could be midnight and he might suddenly want to be at home and in his own bed, and I'd need you to drive us home."

"Not a problem," Cade drawled, and shrugged, putting a handful of bills on the table for the waitress. "I like driving at night."

For some reason his shrug and easy answer bothered her. It was a little too easy, a little too smooth. She flashed to David, and then she knew why she'd gotten her back up. David had been the same way…slick, charming, telling her only what he thought she wanted to hear. But Rachel wasn't interested in smooth or charming. She wanted true. She wanted honest. And she wanted real.

"You better mean that, Cade," she said fiercely, her tone suddenly flinty.

"Mean what, Rache?"

"Everything." Her jaw jutted and her eyes locked with his. "Because I'd rather you just take us home tonight than say things you don't mean."

Chapter Seven

Rachel's heart pounded as Cade drove them back to his ranch house. She couldn't believe she'd agreed to this. She shouldn't have agreed, but Tommy was happy, humming to himself in the backseat of the cab. He remained in a buoyant mood at the ranch house where he followed Cade around the barn as he checked on each horse and then returned to the house to feed Lacey.

But by eight Tommy was nearly asleep among the puppies, and Rachel carefully disentangled him from wriggling golden puppies and rubber dog toys.

Cade had shown them around the house earlier today and had given them the big guest bedroom at the end of the hall downstairs. All the other bedrooms were upstairs but Rachel had been worried about Tommy and the stairs.

"Tommy, can you say good-night to Cade?" she said, pausing, waiting for him to respond, just as she always did. It's what the speech therapist had taught her. Include him in your conversations. Give him an opportunity to speak. Give him verbal cues. And so she did. But unlike most nights when he ignored her or retreated to silence, he spoke.

"Night," he said haltingly, smiling briefly, the smile sliding over his face before it was gone. "Cade. Cade."

Cade smiled back, his expression gentle. "Night, buddy. Sleep good."

She reached for Tommy's hand but he pulled away and looked at Cade. His hand twisted in the air. "Horses," he said. His hand waved up and down in a swimming motion.

Cade nodded, understanding without needing Rachel to translate. "That's right, Tommy. I promised you we'd see the horses again, and we will, in the morning." Cade glanced at her, his expression impossible to read. "And if your mom agrees, I'll take you on a horseback ride."

Both Tommy and Cade turned to look at her and Rachel struggled to hide her dismay. "Horseback ride?"

Cade nodded casually. "Tommy thought it sounded like fun."

"He doesn't know how to ride," she answered under her breath, aware that Tommy was watching her face carefully.

"He likes horses, Rachel."

"They're huge," she said, smiling tightly.

"And he's not afraid of them." Cade hesitated and glanced down at Tommy, picking his words with care. "I've been reading up, you know, trying to learn about autism, and studies show that children on the autism spectrum respond well to horses and dogs. They're both frequently used in animal-assisted therapy, and all over the country horseback riding is a common form of therapy for children with autism."

Rachel wasn't sure she liked Cade telling her what was good for Tommy. Tommy was her son. She was responsible for him. And while she appreciated Cade being kind to Tommy, as well as exposing him to new things, she worried that Tommy was becoming too attached to Cade, forming a bond with someone who wouldn't be able to keep the promises he'd made to her son. Because let's face it. Cade had disappeared on her before. He could very easily fall off the wagon and then he'd be disappearing on her—them—again.

Cade must have read her resistance because he pressed his case. "Horseback riding can help children with their physical development. It'll strengthen muscles and improve coordination. But it's also something fun. It'd give him pleasure. And I think it's good for him to be out of doors, in fresh air, doing new things—" He broke off, his gaze searching her face, and then he sighed and shrugged. "But you're his mom. You know what's best for him. Obviously, I'd never have Tommy do something you don't approve of."

Slightly mollified, she gave Cade a brief nod. "Thank you," she said, before steering Tommy out of the room and walking him down the hall to the guest room where she and Tommy would be sharing the queen-size bed.

After washing his hands and face at the sink in the attached bathroom, she tucked her little boy into bed and stayed with him until he was asleep. It usually took fifteen or twenty minutes for him to fall asleep, but tonight Tommy was so excited from his day, as well as overtired, that it was almost an hour before he wound down, giving Rachel far too much time to just lie there in the dark and think.

And she didn't want to think, not about Cade, or how she felt when around him, or even the fact that he'd been doing research on autism, because it impressed her. As well as troubled her. On one hand she was glad that he'd taken interest in Tommy, and Tommy's unique and challenging world, but on the other hand, she knew how easy it was to get swept up in Cade's warmth and charisma, and she never wanted Tommy hurt the way she'd been hurt.

Maybe she should limit the amount of time Tommy spent with Cade. Or maybe she needed to make it clear to Cade that Tommy wasn't a cute puppy looking to be adopted by a loving cowboy. No, he was a boy, a complex little boy with lots of special needs, which included needing to be protected from people who might abruptly abandon him…

A door banged in a distant part of the house and Rachel sat up, rubbing her eyes. She'd dozed off waiting for Tommy to sleep and she glanced now at the bedside clock. Ten. Time for her to go to sleep herself, except that suddenly she wasn't tired anymore. Leaving the bed, she dragged a hand through her hair and opened the bedroom door.

The house was dark, with just a few lights on here and there, and those that had been left on were dim. Cade must have gone to bed, she thought, peeking into the family room where Lacey and her pups were sleeping. But Lacey heard her and she lifted her head and whined softly. Rachel went to her, gave her back a scratch, whispering thanks in her ear for being so nice to Tommy, before heading to the kitchen to make a cup of tea.

In the kitchen, Rachel flicked on the overhead light and froze as she spotted Cade by the stove, leaning against a counter. He'd changed from jeans into soft, baggy, gray sweatpants that hung low on his hips and a short-sleeve, black T-shirt that stretched tight over his big biceps. His feet were bare. His dark hair was slightly rumpled, and she didn't think he'd ever looked better. Or sexier.

"I'm sorry," she said, gulping a breath and hanging back in the doorway. "I didn't know you were in here."

"Just making a cup of tea," he said, nodding at the kettle on the stove. "Want one?"

"Yes, please."

"Water should boil soon. Come in. Sit."

Rachel hesitated, suddenly overwhelmed by the domesticity of the scene.

If he hadn't loved his liquor…

If they'd stayed together…

This was how it would have been with them. Intimate, warm, sweet…very sweet, because she would have loved nothing more than coming downstairs to him every night after putting their babies to bed. She would have loved walking into the kitchen and seeing him here in his pajamas, gorgeous and sexy and ready for bed…

Don't go there, she told herself, catching herself. *Don't get tangled up in a fantasy that is only a fantasy…you have to know it would have never been like that. He's good at wooing and winning, but he's not a man who can keep the promises he makes…*

And yet, what if he had changed? What if things could be different this time?

As if reading her mind again, Cade gave her a wry smile and crooked his finger, beckoning her. "Come, darlin'. I might bark, but I don't bite."

She blushed and fidgeted with the string at the neckline of her peasant blouse. "You used to bite."

His smile stretched, his blue eyes warm. "That's right. And you, darlin', used to like it."

Rachel's eyes widened and she gulped, growing warmer by the moment because yes, it had been good with them. Very good. And she'd once thought that maybe it was this way for everyone, but then she'd slept with David and it hadn't been the same.

"Sorry. I don't remember," she said with a careless shrug, jamming her hands in the back pockets of her jeans.

"Liar," he teased.

She shrugged again, feigning indifference.

He laughed softly, studying her from beneath his lashes. "You're not scared to be alone with me, are you?"

Rachel went hot, then cold, and her tummy did a crazy little flip. *"No."*

"Uh-huh."

Her cheekbones burned and she lifted her chin to hide the fact that she was nervous and excited and just a little bit turned on. "I'm not."

"Yes, you are."

"I'm not."

He gestured to the chair at the table. "Then come in. Have a seat. I promise I won't eat you."

Her face burned. "Barking. Biting. Eating. What are you, auditioning for the part of the wolf in 'Little Red Riding Hood'?"

"If you're Little Red Riding Hood," he said lazily, shifting his weight against the counter.

The subtle shift of his hips caught her attention and her gaze dropped to the skin suddenly visible just above the low, loose drawstring waist of his sweats and below the hem of his T-shirt. It was only a couple inches, but what a view... hard carved abs and the tantalizing jut of hip bones.

Her mouth went dry and she went weak in the knees, imagining the feel of his hips against hers, and how good he'd feel, and how warm his skin would be...

It'd been forever since she'd been held. Forever since she'd been loved. Five years and forever...

She shivered, hit by the strongest wave of desire.

The kettle came to a boil, whistling softly. She heard the whistle in a distant part of her brain. "I don't need tea. I think I'll just turn in."

"I probably shouldn't have told you about crashing my truck," he said abruptly. "But I meant what I said about not drinking anymore. I'm done with alcohol. I've given up drinking for good."

"That's great."

"I miss you, Rachel."

She closed her eyes and held her breath, aching on the inside. Finally. Finally, he'd said what she'd waited so long to hear, so why didn't she feel better? She ought to be vindicated, but instead she just felt bruised. Undone.

The kettle whistle turned shrill.

He ignored it. "Give me a chance—"

"Cade, the kettle. Please."

She watched as he grabbed the faded red pot holder and lifted the kettle from the burner. "What kind of tea do you want?" he asked quietly. "Black tea, green tea, herbal?"

She heard the weariness in his voice and the hurt, and her stomach knotted, even as her gaze settled on his hard profile. Once she'd loved to kiss the strong angles and planes of his face, remembering how she'd lavished extra kisses on the scar near the bridge of his nose. "Decaf or herbal. Or I won't be able to sleep."

Silently he took two mugs from the cupboard over his head and she watched as he pried the lid off a large tin filled with boxes of tea, selecting a couple tea bags and dropping one in each cup.

He added hot water, and then carried the steaming mugs to the table. "Do you want sugar or sweetener?" he asked.

She shook her head. "No, thank you."

He nodded and pulled out one of the ladder-back chairs at the farm table and sat down. "You don't need to stay. You can take your tea to your room. You'll probably relax better there."

She'd wanted to go. She'd been thinking she'd rather drink her tea in her room, but now that he'd said it out loud, she felt ungrateful and mean. Cade had been nothing but kind to her since showing up on her doorstep last Friday. For the past five days he'd picked her up and driven her around, and had been so very patient with Tommy...

"I'm afraid," she blurted.

His jaw dropped. "Of me?"

She nodded jerkily. "But not just afraid of you. I'm afraid of me. Afraid of my judgment in men."

"We were good in the beginning," he said softly.

"I know we were, and I know it was your...past...catching up with you that made you drink, but David..." She shuddered. "David...he was just bad news from the be-ginning, and I was so determined to turn him into you—"

"He was a cowboy?"

She laughed hollowly. "No, a salesman, and he sold me." She shook her head, lips compressing. "But that's not fair. I knew he was too smooth and slick, but I let him sell me any-way, convincing myself that because he was tall, with dark hair and blue eyes, he was like you. But he wasn't. He was shallow and fake, completely insincere. And when we.... did it, it was awful. Empty and disgusting and I hated the way he touched me."

Cade said nothing and she didn't blame him. This wasn't easy to talk about, but it was something she wanted him to know.

Rachel joined him at the table, sitting in a chair opposite Cade's. She pulled the mug toward her, her hands lightly circling the hot exterior. "Needless to say, there was only that one time. It had been a horrible experience in my mind, and I wanted nothing to do with him, which was good as I think he was just as disappointed by me." She paused and glanced down into her cup, breathing in the sweet fruity aroma of her tea. Peach or mango, or maybe a combination of the two. "Imagine my surprise when I discovered eight weeks later that I was pregnant. I was so upset. I wanted to die. I thought my life was over."

She glanced up and saw that Cade was watching her in-tently, his expression pained, and she didn't blame him. This was hard. This was pretty darn gritty stuff and she didn't like it, wasn't proud of it, but it was part of her past, part of who she was, and it's where Tommy had come from. This was his beginning, how he was made, and Cade needed to understand that becoming a single mother had broken what was left of her heart.

Rachel exhaled slowly. "Grandma was a rock and a saint,

and sometimes a saint throwing rocks. She sat me down and told me I had two choices. I could take the money David had given me for an abortion and get the abortion, or I could grow up and take responsibility for my actions and become the best mom I could be. So I became Tommy's mom, and it was the best decision I ever made."

"You made the right decision."

"Not everyone thinks so, but I don't care what they think, and I've given up trying to prove anything to anyone. Now it's about doing what works for us, doing what's right for us. Making Tommy healthy and happy."

"You're a great mom."

Her eyes burned and she twisted her shoulders. "At the end of the day, I get tired. I lose my temper. But then I go to sleep and I wake up ready to try again the next day."

"Not your average girl," he said quietly, reaching across the table to lightly touch her cheek.

It was a brief caress, fleeting, really, but it was enough to make her feel fragile, beautiful, special. For a moment she almost felt like his girl again, the one who'd once been so sure they could get through anything that life sent their way.

"I've made mistakes," she said huskily.

Cade nodded, expression somber. "Haven't we all, darlin'?"

Chapter Eight

Cade slept fitfully, aware that Rachel was in his house, beneath his roof. He wanted her so much that when he woke yet again, this time at five-thirty, he climbed out of bed and stepped into jeans, snapping the fly front over his boxers, despite the fact that it was pitch-dark outside and would be for at least another hour. Cade tugged an old black thermal shirt over his head, the material shrunk and faded from repeated washings, before adding a flannel shirt over that for warmth, but this, too, was soft and comfortable, something he needed after a night without rest.

Grooming was easy. After combing his hair and brushing his teeth, Cade skipped the shave. He didn't have the patience to do a decent job and wasn't in the mood to nick his chin.

Grimly, Cade stared at his reflection, focusing on the fine wrinkles fanning from his eyes and the deep lines etched on either side of his mouth. He looked about as old as he felt this morning. A hell of a lot older than thirty-three. But older was good, he reminded himself. Older meant wiser.

Downstairs Cade let out Lacey, made a pot of coffee, put out fresh water and food for Lacey, then stared out the window at the morning waiting for the coffee to finish brewing. He drank a cup scalding hot and black before heading to his barn and grabbing supplies to mend a fence he should have fixed a week ago but hadn't.

Now parking at the top of a hill a few miles from the ranch house, the sun was just flirting with the morning, turning a slice of sky pale yellow with light. Tugging on his work gloves, Cade cast the dawn one last glance, wondering what the day would bring, before slinging a big ball of barbwire out of the back of the truck and carrying the wire to the fence. He'd left his truck's headlights on to give him light to work by, but even with the dark and the frigid temperature, this was work he could practically do in his sleep.

As the sky lightened, turning pale blue with a few wispy pink clouds, Cade paused to rub at his hands, which ached from the chill, and found himself thinking of Rachel yet again, and didn't she just tangle him up even more than this bundle of barbwire?

Rachel and Tommy had only been here a day but he liked having them here. Liked it a lot. It felt right to climb from bed and go to work, knowing they were still in their beds, sleeping. Somehow in just one day they'd taken his big empty house and made it feel like a home. The kind of home he'd always wanted as a kid. Now he just needed to figure out how to convince Rachel that she and Tommy belonged here, too. Permanently.

He pulled out a nail from his pocket and, slamming the hammer down, attached the corner of the wire to the top of the post, before working his way down the post, nail by nail, until the entire length was secure.

Beads of perspiration formed on his brow, dampening the brim of his hat. He welcomed the work and the burn in his muscles, welcomed the distraction. He'd rather wrestle the fence than his emotions, especially this ache of desire. He wanted to make love to her, yes, but this need he felt was more than sex, it was about holding her, loving her, letting her know he'd changed.

And he had changed. She just didn't know it yet.

Another truck bounced up the rough dirt road, kicking up clouds of dust. The truck parked and a grizzled old cowboy swung out of the cab, walking toward Cade with the bowlegged gait of a man who'd spent his life in the saddle.

"Need a hand, boss?" the cowboy asked, putting on his own leather gloves.

"Morning, Bill," Cade grunted around the three nails in his teeth as his ranch foreman straightened out the length of wire and tugged it tight so Cade could hammer this next section down.

"Stopped by the house," the foreman said.

Cade hammered the top down. "Uh-huh."

"Met Rachel."

"Yeah," Cade said, knowing that Bill had heard him talk about Rachel plenty of times over the years.

"Is that her boy?"

"Yeah."

Bill hesitated, and Cade glanced up at him from beneath the brim of his hat, holding his foreman's gaze. Bill van Zandt had been the first person Cade had hired after buying Sweetwater three years ago with his saved rodeo winnings, and the best person he'd ever hired, but Cade wouldn't tolerate disrespect from Bill or anyone else who worked for him. "You got any other questions, van Zandt?"

"Is he yours?" Bill asked bluntly.

"No."

"Who is the dad?"

"Some loser who walked away from Rachel when she needed him most," Cade said tersely, tugging on the fence, checking to see if the section was attached securely, before heading to the next post.

Bill wisely dropped the questions as they finished repairing the fence in silence, but Cade couldn't quiet the taunting voice in his head, the one that was saying he and Rachel's loser boyfriend had a lot in common. They'd both walked away from Rachel, choosing to take the easy way out instead of doing the right thing. Fortunately, there was one huge difference—Cade loved Rachel, and this time he was fighting for her. And not just Rachel, but Tommy, too.

Returning to the ranch house, Cade headed to the kitchen to pour a cup of coffee and warm up his frozen hands. He stomped his feet on the mat outside the mudroom door and peeled off his sheepskin jacket, hanging it on a hook by the back door.

Entering the kitchen, he discovered Rachel already there, standing at the counter in front of the coffeepot. She jumped and turned to face him, her expression almost guilty. "I just started a fresh pot. Hope that's okay."

He drank her in, thinking she looked almost as pretty as she had that first day in her yellow sundress. "That's great," he said, smiling, knowing he was smiling and unable to help it. She was wearing the big flannel robe he'd given her last night before she'd turned in, and she'd twisted her dark hair into a loose knot on top of her head, the dark heavy mass anchored by a yellow pencil, but already tendrils were falling out, tumbling around her pink cheeks. What he wouldn't give to pick her up and carry her into his bedroom right now.

Her cheeks turned a darker pink and she tugged the edges of the robe closer together, making the shapeless, sacklike robe even more modest, and he grinned. "You're gorgeous, Rachel. I don't think I've ever seen you look better," he said, going to the sink to wash his hands, letting the hot water warm his stiff joints and fingers.

She rolled her eyes and tucked one of those sexy tendrils of hair behind her ear. "Nonsense."

"I'm serious." He turned the water off and grabbed a towel to dry his hands before facing her. "You've got to be the prettiest girl in all of Texas."

"Now you're just talking to hear yourself talk."

"Is that so?"

"Mmm-hmm."

"Then maybe it's time I stopped talking and showed you what I'm feeling."

Her gray eyes warmed, sparking with a fire he didn't think he'd ever see again, before she smashed it down, hiding her emotions and passion behind that wall of cordiality she maintained around him. "I don't think so," she said primly, firmly, and he was amused.

He liked challenges. He was a professional cowboy for Pete's sake. He had no problem proving himself over and over and over. It's who he was. It's what he did.

"Why are you smiling?" she demanded, pressing the flannel robe to her breast.

He tried so hard not to look at that lucky breast. He remembered how soft she was and sweet and lovely—

"Cade," she said, calling him back to the moment.

"Yes, darlin'?"

"I'm not your darling."

"Yes, you are."

"I'm not."

"You are."

"I bet you call every girl 'darlin'.'"

"No, ma'am." He shook his head and walked toward her slowly, his arms relaxed at his sides. It was the same way he approached skittish mares, showing them he had nothing in his hands, nothing to frighten them. Rachel's eyes widened, watching him approach, and she would have backed up if she could, but there was nowhere for her to go. She was stuck in a corner between counters and that coffee machine puffing away as it brewed a delicious-smelling pot of coffee.

"You should stop right there," she said breathlessly.

"Right where?" he asked innocently, taking another step toward her, perfectly aware that he'd already covered the floor and if he reached out now, he'd have no problem touching her.

She tipped her head back to look up into his eyes. Damn, but she was just a little thing, just reaching his shoulder in bare feet. He'd forgotten how small she was, how delicate and lovely, and gazing down into her wide eyes, he saw that they had darkened, the gray irises reminding him of storm clouds. Gray eyes with flecks of sea-green and black…

Rachel held her breath, lost in Cade's eyes. His eyes weren't just blue, they were electric-blue and full of fire, and she knew what he was thinking, knew he wanted to kiss her.

Her skin prickled, the hair on her nape rising as he slowly leaned in to her, slowly enough to give her every chance to stop him. He was making it perfectly clear that he wouldn't kiss her if she didn't want him to. He wouldn't force a kiss on her. He wanted her willing, and she was willing. And so she didn't stop him. Instead she waited, hands balled in the pockets of his robe, heart thumping, blood racing in her veins.

She wanted this kiss. Needed this kiss. Needed to know if she'd imagined how good it'd felt being kissed by Cade King…

His dark head dipped and his blue eyes flashed, locking with hers for the briefest second before his mouth covered hers, his lips firm and cool, almost cold from having been outside, and yet it was exactly right, familiar and good, this man with his firm, cool lips and strong, beard-roughened jaw. A shiver raced through her and she sighed with pleasure, lips parting beneath his.

He deepened the kiss just as slowly, and again she was the one who moved toward him, pressing closer, wanting more, knowing this was how a kiss should be.

After what seemed like a very long time, he lifted his head and stared down into her eyes. But it was hard to focus on anything when her legs were so weak and her belly felt as if it was flipping inside and out as pleasure surged through her.

"Wow," she whispered, licking her bottom lip, which was tingling like mad, as was the rest of her. "Apparently some things haven't changed."

His lips curved but his blue eyes didn't smile. Instead they burned with a fire she couldn't identify. "The good parts of me are still here. It's the drunk ass that's gone."

She lifted a hand to his face, her fingertips gently touching his hard, carved cheekbone, and then down to the new scar just under his chin. "I once loved you more than anything."

His gaze searched hers. "I know I don't have any right to be back in your life, Rache, but I want a chance to prove to you I'm different—"

He stepped even closer, narrowing the distance between them to a hairbreadth.

Her heart hammered as he gazed down into her eyes, drinking his fill before slowly, carefully, tucking one of her tendrils of hair behind her ear. "I was a fool to leave you," he said, the backs of his fingers brushing the curve of her cheekbone and then along her jaw.

Rachel shivered at his touch.

"Hands down, the biggest mistake of my life," he added.

"You broke my heart," she whispered, her breath catching in her throat as her body seemed to hum, remembering him. Crazy how she only needed a touch and she was his again, her pulse pounding, the blood singing in her veins.

"Leaving you broke mine, too. Nothing was the same without you. Life didn't mean anything without you." He tucked another tendril of hair behind her ear, his fingertips tracing the shell of her ear and then moving lower to the little hollow beneath the lobe. "You're so soft, so sweet."

Then Cade dropped his head, and his mouth touched hers in a slow, lingering kiss that sent darts of feeling from her nipples to her belly and beyond.

Cade deepened the kiss, one of his hands cupping the back of her head so he could angle his mouth even closer, while the other settled in the small of her back, molding her body to his. He was warm and real, and suddenly she couldn't get close enough. Rachel stood up on tiptoe to wrap her arms around his neck, pressing herself closer, loving how his big, hard body felt against hers. Instinctively her fingers curled into the cool crisp hair at his collar, savoring the silky texture and the warmth of his skin at his nape. "You feel so good," she whispered against his mouth.

"I think it'd feel even better without so many clothes on."

She drew back to look up into his blue eyes, and they were bright, hot and hungry. "I don't remember that part in 'Little Red Riding Hood.'"

"This is the adult version."

"Ah." Her lips twitched as she fought a smile.

"Is that a problem?"

"Not necessarily." Rachel hesitated. "Tommy shouldn't wake up for another hour."

His burning gaze held hers. "Are you saying what I think you're saying?"

"I've missed you, Cade."

His smile slipped and pain shadowed eyes. "Darlin', if I could go back in time and fix everything, I would."

"Was I that easy to leave?"

"Walking away from you was the hardest thing I've ever done."

"You didn't come back."

"Took me a while to get sober. And then it's taken me a while to make peace with myself for being a loser—"

"You were never a loser, Cade. You just had demons—"

He cut off her words with another kiss, even fiercer this time, his lips parting hers, his tongue tracing the softness of her upper lip and then the fullness of the lower lip, before slipping deeper inside to tease her tongue. Rachel's belly clenched with need and she pressed her hips against Cade's, rubbing up against the hard ridge in his jeans. "Have somewhere more private we could go?" she asked.

"I've got a big bed in my room, but it's upstairs."

"We can leave the door open."

"And you really think we've got an hour?"

"More like fifty-seven minutes now."

"That settles that," Cade said, easily swinging her up into his arms and carrying her out of the kitchen and up the stairs to the master bedroom, where he set her down on his bed before gently pressing her back against the mattress to kiss the side of her neck. "Can't believe you're really here."

"Neither can I," she breathed, as he pushed back the edges of her robe to kiss her collarbone and then a little lower. "Is this crazy?"

He'd been kissing his way down the slope of her breast and he flicked his tongue across her pert nipple before lifting his head to look her in the eye. "No, darlin'. I think this is the first sane thing I've done in years. You're my girl. You'll always be my girl."

And then he was untying the sash of her robe and kissing her and stroking her everywhere until she didn't want anything but him. At her urging, Cade sheathed himself with a condom and settled between her thighs, and when he entered her, Rachel didn't think she'd ever felt anything half so good in her entire life.

They made love the way she remembered…slowly, hungrily, with passion and need. And it might have been more than five years since they'd last made love, but Cade knew how to touch her and satisfy her, and he made sure she found release before he did.

Afterward, Rachel lay sleepy and relaxed in his arms, her cheek against his chest, listening to the strong, even thud of his heartbeat.

"Regrets?" Cade asked, his voice deep and slightly uncertain.

Her heart turned over. "No. I love being with you."

"It feels right, doesn't it?"

"It does—" And then she stopped at the sound of a door opening downstairs. "Tommy."

"I heard him, too," Cade said, slipping out from beneath her and leaving the bed to step into his boxers and jeans.

Rachel slipped into her robe, tying the sash tightly around her waist as she headed for the stairs with Cade close on her heels, but before she could take a step down, Cade caught her in his arms and spun her around to face him. "That was amazing," he said, dropping a quick kiss on her lips. "You are amazing."

She smiled and blushed. "It was pretty good, wasn't it?"

"Next time we get together, though, it's going to be a real date. Dinner, dancing, the works."

"I'll hold you to that," she teased as he let her go, and she skipped down the stairs with him close on her heels.

They found Tommy sitting on the family-room floor with Lacey and the pups. "Dog," Tommy said happily, smiling up at them as they entered the room. "Puppies. Tommy's puppies. Yes?"

Chapter Nine

Cade walked Tommy's pony around the corral on a lead, and even though Milly was slow, sweet and placid, Tommy was thrilled, his eyes wide, his lips parted in an ecstatic O.

Rachel perched on the top rail of the corral, watching her boy circle around, his small back straight, his little hands clutching the pommel, and she could tell from the way he smiled that this was heaven. Life couldn't get any better for him, and she'd seen a different boy here. One less anxious, one less detached and distracted, one more interested in the world around him. It was the ranch and the animals, but also Cade. He'd worked some kind of magic—just how or what she didn't know.

Maybe he had started to grow his wings.

And around and around they went for nearly an hour with Tommy beaming the entire time, happy, so very, very happy.

How was she ever going to tear him away from this place?

She glanced at Cade, and her gaze took in his broad shoulders and strong, muscular legs, and she wondered how she'd ever leave him, because he'd worked his magic on her, too. But had he really changed? Could he be trusted? Could he be trusted with her son as well as her heart? She hoped so, but to be honest, she didn't know. It was one of those things that only time would tell.

"Okay, last time around, Tommy," Rachel heard Cade tell Tommy from the far side of the corral, "and then I've got to check on my cows before we take your mom to get her car."

To Rachel's surprise, Tommy didn't protest about getting off the horse, and it wasn't until he was pointing at Cade's truck that she understood why. It turned out Cade had promised Tommy that he could ride along with him when Cade went to check on his cows in the west pasture.

"We won't be long. I just want to make sure the new fence is holding. We'll be gone twenty to thirty minutes at the most. Do you want to come?" Cade asked her.

Rachel hadn't seen much of the ranch and would enjoy a drive, especially on a clear-sky day like today, but she'd had a call earlier from a couple wanting to book her for their wedding cake and she needed to phone the bride-to-be back. "I actually need to return a call. Are you comfortable taking Tommy on your own?"

"Of course," Cade answered, lifting Tommy into the truck and buckling him into his booster seat.

She glanced at Tommy, who was staring off into space, a vacant expression in his eyes, lost again in his own world. "He should be okay with you," she said.

"He'll be fine with me." Cade leaned over and kissed her forehead. "Don't worry."

Rachel crossed her arms over her chest, fighting to suppress her fear. She was overprotective. Always had been. "See you soon?"

Cade laughed softly as he opened the truck door and climbed behind the steering wheel. "Relax. Nothing's going to happen."

BUT HE WAS WRONG, CADE THOUGHT, thirty-some minutes later. Something had happened. Tommy had vanished.

Cade spun at the top of the hill, his gaze searching

through the scraggly shrubs and clustered oak trees for a little boy in a puffy blue jacket, but there was no sign of Tommy, or his bright blue jacket, anywhere.

Where was he? How could he have vanished? Cade had only turned his back for a minute—just long enough to hammer a couple more nails into a fence post—and when he'd finished hammering the fourth nail, he'd turned and called for Tommy, but Tommy didn't answer. And when Cade returned to the truck to search the cab, Tommy wasn't there, either.

Where could he have gone?

Cade tried not to think of all the streams and ponds on his property. Or the water troughs in every pasture. And then there were the hills with steep banks and jagged drop-offs. The holes that could swallow a small boy…

Cade reached for his walkie-talkie since his cell phone didn't get the best service on his ranch and called Bill, his foreman. "I need you to go to my house and get Rachel. She's on a call and doesn't know you're coming. You need to keep her calm and quickly bring her to me. I'm at the top of the hill overlooking the west pasture, where I was mending the fence earlier this morning—"

"Why do I need to keep her calm? What's going on?"

"I've lost her son. I lost Tommy."

RACHEL WOULD NEVER FORGET the next sixty minutes. She and Cade and Bill van Zandt tramped up and down the hills searching for Tommy. Rachel and Cade constantly called to him. Bill just hunted, inspecting every tree and rotted log and flattened bit of grass, checking for footprints without finding a single one.

The lack of footprints troubled Bill and he told Rachel it didn't make sense. If there was no sign of Tommy's footsteps leaving the grassy hilltop, perhaps he hadn't walked away from the truck. Perhaps he was still in the truck…hiding.

Rachel ran all the way back to Cade's truck because Bill's words had struck a chord. Tommy liked to hide. He loved to play hide-and-seek. What if he'd tried to play hide-and-seek in the truck and gotten himself stuck somewhere? What if he'd gotten wedged in, or the strings on his jacket hood had gotten tangled on something…what if…

Bill radioed Cade as she ran, and Cade reached the truck before she did. Rachel reached the truck to find Cade searching behind the cab seat, and then crawling beneath the truck frame. He was under the truck for what seemed like forever before he let out a shout. "He's here!"

Rachel's legs nearly gave out as she leaned against the truck. "Is he okay?"

"He's not moving," Cade said shortly. "But he's breathing."

"What do you mean, he's not moving?"

"I think…I think he's asleep."

Bill arrived then, and together they worked to ease Tommy out. "He'd wedged himself behind one of the tires," Cade said as he settled a grease-stained Tommy into her arms. "But he doesn't look hurt."

Cade was right. Tommy seemed fine. Rachel, however, was not. She held Tommy on her lap during the short drive back to the ranch house, and then after inspecting Tommy once again in the driveway of Cade's house, asked Cade to take them to her car now.

Cade shot Rachel a dozen different glances during the twenty-minute drive to Weatherford, but she never once looked at him or spoke to him, keeping her gaze averted and on the barren landscape outside his truck window.

"I'm sorry," Cade repeated, having apologized at the top

of the hill and then again in his driveway. "It shouldn't have happened. I should have watched him better—"

"Yes, and you're right," she said tightly, cutting him short, unable to bear yet another apology because Cade didn't get it. What had just happened was potentially tragic and fatal. If he'd climbed behind the wheel and returned to the ranch to get her, if he'd driven his truck any distance— She shuddered. "It shouldn't have happened. And you should have watched him better."

"I thought he was right there behind me."

"But he wasn't."

"I only turned my back for a minute."

She shot Tommy a quick glance over her shoulder. He was staring out the window, oblivious to everything, and at this moment, Rachel was grateful for that, but she dropped her voice anyway. "He could have died, Cade."

"I *know.*"

She shook her head and bundled her arms across her chest, biting back the furious retorts that rose to her lips, because he didn't know. Cade thought he knew, but he didn't know, and that's how Tommy had gotten lost in the first place. Children had to be watched. Children needed vigilant, attentive parents. Parents who wouldn't get distracted. Parents who put their children's needs first, and their own needs second.

And the truth was, while she was upset with Cade, she was even more upset with herself. What was she thinking, sending Tommy off with Cade? Cade had never been a father. He didn't know the first thing about raising children. But she did. And she knew Tommy wasn't an easy child to manage. She'd known that he could be a handful, and yet she'd allowed inexperienced Cade to take her son with him...

Rachel was grateful to arrive at Phil's auto shop, and she

held on to Tommy's hand while she paid Phil, and Cade quietly transferred Tommy's booster seat from his truck into the back of Rachel's Jeep.

Once the bill was settled, she put her purse into the car and buckled Tommy into his seat, aware that Cade was standing at her side, silently watching, waiting for her to finish so they could…what? Talk? And yet what was there to say? Was there anything for them to say? They'd made a mistake. This wasn't going to work. She should have used better judgment…because truly, she had known better.

And that's what she ended up saying to him—in pretty much those words. He hadn't flinched at her announcement—thank God—but she could tell she'd struck a nerve, and she watched the emotion fade from his eyes and saw his strong jaw harden.

She gulped a breath, determined to get through this, and put an end to this once and for all. "So I don't think we should see each other again," she concluded lamely, shriveling a little under his now-glacier gaze. "I'm sorry. But I have to think of Tommy. Do what's best for him."

"And I'm not best for him."

She winced at his harsh tone. "I didn't say that."

"But that's what you mean, isn't it?" His powerful shoulders shifted, his jaw jutting. "I don't come from a great family. I haven't had a lot of experience with kids. So no, I'm not daddy material, but I do care about him, Rache. And I care about you—"

"Caring isn't enough. Words don't matter. It's one's actions that matter. It's the actions that count."

Cade looked away, and he ground his teeth together so hard that a small muscle in his jaw popped. "I thought… I wanted…" He shrugged and shook his head. "It doesn't matter what I thought, because you're right. Of course you're right. I'm not a parent. I don't know how to take care of a child with special needs. Christ, I'm the guy that grew up in foster care. Don't trust your child with me."

And then he was walking away from her. Again.

Rachel watched him go, too stunned to speak. He was ending it with her? He wasn't going to even fight for her?

Would he never fight for her?

She exhaled in a painful rush, her eyes stinging, her chest aching, and climbed into her car to leave Cade and the garage behind.

She refused to glance in the rearview mirror, refused to let herself feel anything. She couldn't afford to feel anything, because if she did, she'd realize her heart was close to breaking...

It was at that very moment that Tommy realized they were in her old car and Cade wasn't with them, and he let out one of his ear-piercing shrieks.

"Cade!" Tommy cried, his thin arm jerking, swinging wildly, gesturing back to the garage and Cade's truck as she merged with traffic on the road.

Rachel sucked in a breath, fingers tightening around the steering wheel. "He's got to go work," she said, trying to sound calm, unruffled, even though her insides were lurching and her eyes were burning and all she wanted to do was cry. "And we do, too, honey. We need to go home and finish packing—"

"Cade house. Cade. Go. Mama."

"We can't. We've got to go home, to our house."

"Cade house. Dogs. Mama."

"Maybe someday we can get a dog—"

Tommy made an inarticulate sound, part yelp, part cry of protest, and her eyes burned with tears she wouldn't cry. She was doing the right thing, ending things, going home now, going back to her life. It wouldn't have ever worked with Cade. She knew it, and he knew it, too. Maybe one day they could be friends, but that time wasn't now.

Tommy yelped again, louder this time. "Cade!"

"He's going to go back to the ranch to work, Tommy—"

"Cade!"

Rachel clamped her jaw tight and gripped the steering wheel tighter. And then Tommy began to shriek, that blood-curdling shriek he did that went on forever, and it took every bit of Rachel's strength to keep from crying as she drove them home. Stupid Cade. Stupid, stupid, stupid Cade. And stupid Rachel for loving him in the first place.

It was seven-thirty in the evening and Tommy was finally, thankfully, asleep, after hours of banging and crying and screaming. Thank God they hadn't moved into the apartment yet. Neighbors would have been complaining after the first hour, never mind the next six and a half.

Exhausted, Rachel went through the house, locking doors, pulling blinds on the quiet night. The floorboards creaked beneath her bare feet as she hesitated outside Tommy's room, resting one hand on his closed door.

Their lives—never easy, rarely calm—felt overwhelming right now. It didn't help that there was so much that was unknown…big questions and little questions. But the question that haunted Rachel most was the one about Tommy's future. Would he ever be able to live independently? Would he ever be able to communicate with the world…function in the world?

And if he wouldn't ever be independent, what would happen to him if something happened to her?

Who would care for Tommy if she couldn't?

She'd never thought about his future quite like that before and it was frightening. Because even if she wanted to do it all on her own, she couldn't. Tommy needed more than her.

He needed a family…a mom and a dad, brothers and sisters, people who would love him and protect him. And maybe it was selfish, but she wanted to be part of a family, too.

For a moment there, she'd imagined starting that family with Cade…

Crazy, silly her. Crazy, silly her for hoping…wanting… needing…

Rachel turned out the hall light and went to her room and changed into pajamas and brushed her teeth for bed. But once in bed she couldn't sleep. All she could think about, all she could see, was Cade.

Cade.

All-Around Cowboy. Broken cowboy. And keeper of her heart.

The days crept by, one after the other, Thursday, Friday, and then it was Saturday, and Rachel filled the hours of each day with packing box after box of kitchen utensils, toys, bedding, clothes, towels.

And in between taking care of Tommy and packing up the rest of the house, she told herself she was glad Cade hadn't called, that it was better this way, ending their relationship this way, before things got even more serious, but Tommy didn't seem to think so. He took every opportunity to ask for Cade, and then when she couldn't produce Cade, Tommy had another meltdown, and the meltdowns were wearing Rachel down, so much so that on Saturday afternoon when Tommy started begging for Cade again instead of eating his lunch, she completely lost it with him, shouting back at him that Cade was gone and that he wasn't going to see Cade anymore.

It wasn't the wisest thing to do, nor was it kind, and so Tommy, hurt and frustrated, ran into his room and dumped out his bin of LEGO and then began pelting the walls with handfuls of LEGO pieces.

"Stop it!" she shouted at him.

He ignored her, throwing more at the wall and window.

"Tommy!"

More LEGO went flying.

"Tommy!"

"What's going on?" A deep male voice demanded from the hallway.

Cade?

Rachel stiffened and spun around to face Cade King. "What are you doing here?"

His hands went to his hips as his gaze swept Tommy's LEGO-strewn room. "What's going on in here?"

"You can't just walk into my house," she answered.

"I rang the doorbell. You didn't answer." He glanced at her, a black eyebrow lifting. "But then, it's probably hard to hear the doorbell when you're yelling."

She nodded at Tommy. "He started it."

"But you're the adult."

"I don't want to be the adult anymore. I'm tired of being the adult. I want to have a tantrum now, too."

Cade gave her a strange look and pushed past her to enter Tommy's bedroom. Rachel watched him crouch down next to Tommy and say something to him. Tommy released his handful of LEGO and stared up into Cade's face. "Dog?" he asked hopefully.

Exhausted, Rachel turned away and walked out, leaving Tommy and Cade together in her son's room while she went to the kitchen and then through the kitchen door to the small backyard beyond. She was sitting in Tommy's swing when Cade found her.

"I've never seen you lose it with him before," Cade said.

"He's been having a lot of tantrums lately and I'm tired."

"Why so many tantrums?"

She tilted her head back to look up into Cade's face, and

her heart did a painful twist. She still loved Cade, didn't she? "Tommy wanted you," she said flatly, trying to smile but finding it impossible. "He didn't understand why he couldn't go see you and the dogs."

"Do you want me to try to explain it to him?" Cade offered.

She planted her feet beneath her to keep the swing from moving. "And what would you tell him?"

Cade's broad shoulders shifted. "That I love his momma more than anything, and I want to love him, too—"

"Cade!"

"—and I'm not sure how to be a dad, but I want to try."

"What are you saying?" she whispered, staring up at him as her heart thumped a mile a minute.

He crouched down next to her and placed his hands on either side of her hips on the wooden swing. "I'm a rodeo cowboy, Rache. I get thrown a lot. I spend a lot of time falling on my ass and my head, but I'm not a quitter. And I want another chance. I know I can make this work, Rache, and maybe I haven't got it right yet, but I'll learn. I can. Give me a chance to be the man you deserve."

Rachel stared deep into his eyes, unable to think of a single thing to say. Did he mean it? Could he do it? Could she?

The door opened and Tommy stepped out, a pillow under one arm and a tub of LEGO under the other. "Cade house. Go." He struggled to smile. "Mama. Go. Cade house. House. Home."

Rachel looked from Cade to her son and back again. "You don't understand, Cade. If we go with you to your house, you're never going to get us out again—"

"Good." His lips curved but his eyes didn't smile. Instead they burned with a fierce blue light that made her heart stutter and her tummy flip over. "Because I don't want you anywhere but on my ranch with me."

She searched his eyes some more, and even though part of her wanted to go with him back to his ranch house, she couldn't. She wasn't ready. They weren't ready. There were things they had to work through, things that needed to be discussed. "We can't go home with you," she said quietly, regretfully. "It's too soon, and if things don't work out, it'll just confuse Tommy more."

"Things *will* work out."

"How do we know that? We haven't even had a real date…and you did promise me one. You promised me dinner, dancing, the works."

"Fine. Let's do it."

"When?"

"Wednesday?"

"Wednesday?" Her nose wrinkled. "Why Wednesday?"

"It's Valentine's Day."

MRS. MUNOZ, HAVING BEEN given a clean bill of health, watched Tommy so Cade and Rachel could go out Valentine's Day evening. Rachel dressed simply for their date, wearing a silver-gray turtleneck with dark jeans and a pair of gorgeous gray cowboy boots Cade had given her years ago for her nineteenth birthday.

After picking her up, Cade drove her to one of his favorite restaurants outside Mineral Wells, a folksy place known to locals for its ribs and barbecue. Strings of colored lights glimmered in the oak trees outside the restaurant, and the sound of an amplified fiddle greeted them in the parking lot.

The hostess seated them in a booth not far from the country-and-western band and the sawdust-covered dance floor.

They ordered appetizers and iced tea but barely touched either one. "Not hungry?" Cade asked her as she sipped her iced tea and avoided the food.

"Not really," she confessed.

"Why not?"

"I don't know. I guess I'm too excited just being here with you."

He studied her for a long moment from across the wooden table. "So what do you want in life, Rache? If you could have anything, what would it be?"

Her slim shoulders shrugged. "Family. Love. Happiness."

"Could I be part of that family?"

"I hope so," she said softly.

"You mean that?"

"Tommy already thinks you are."

"And you? What do you think?"

She took her time answering him, suddenly finding it hard to breathe. "You've always been the only one for me."

"Good answer," he said, smiling at her. Then he stood up and reached for Rachel's hand. "Come on. We've got some catching up to do."

She put her hand in his, and Cade walked her backward onto the dance floor, his hips bracing hers. Heat rushed through her, and her cheeks burned hot. Nervous, excited, she tipped her head back to see his face, and his gaze locked with hers. "Remember how to two-step?" he asked, drawing her into his arms.

"I think so," she flashed.

For the next fifteen minutes they danced, dipped and twirled around the dance floor, boots kicking up small clouds of fresh, fragrant sawdust. Cade had always been a good dancer, and in his arms, with the band covering popular country-and-western songs, Rachel felt the years fall away. It was easy being with him, and fun.

Fun.

Good Lord, it'd been a long time since she'd had fun.

The last fast song left them both breathless. Cade spun Rachel around, and she fanned her face. "No more," she begged, struggling to catch her breath and trying desperately to smooth wild tendrils of hair back from her face. "I'm out of shape."

"No, you're not. You feel amazing to me."

Laughing, she batted away his wandering hand. "That's not what I meant, and you know it!"

He laughed, too, and it was a deep sexy sound that rumbled from his chest. The band changed tunes, slowing the tempo, and he drew her back into his arms. "Think you can manage a slow one, old gal?"

She snorted with outrage, and then gave way to a fit of giggles. "I'll try."

"Good girl."

Rachel sighed as he adjusted his stride to hers, fitting her body snugly against his. He knew her so well. It'd been years since they danced, and yet it felt absolutely right…as if they had been made for each other.

But then, they *had* been made for each other. They'd always been right for each other. Unfortunately, they'd allowed life to get in the way but life had brought them back together, and this time they were both older and wiser and they knew what they had.

She knew what they had. And it was good. Better than good. It was special. Magical.

She lifted her head, looked up into his face, and his unwavering gaze met hers and held. "I know what you're thinking," he said, his deep voice so low and husky it felt like fingers caressing her spine. "But I'm not going away, Rache. I've bought a ranch and built a house and I may be a novice when it comes to kids, but I can learn. I can learn to be a good dad, and I am determined to be a great husband, and I'm ready for a family. I've changed, Rachel, I have—"

"I know you have, and I owe you an apology, Cade. I haven't been fair to you—"

"No apology needed. You're a mother, a very good

mother, and you're a proper mama bear, and I love that about you."

"You know he already loves you," she said. "Tommy's never had a father, but he loves you already like you're his daddy—"

"I'm glad, because he's my boy now. And no matter how many kids you and I have, he'll always be my first son."

"You really mean that?"

"Absolutely."

Rachel stopped moving and stared up into his face. "We're going to have kids?"

"Oh, yes. At least, I hope so. I'd love some babies…girl babies that look just like you." Suddenly he was drawing her off the dance floor and out a patio door into the garden where they huddled beneath one of the heat lamps.

"It's freezing out here!" she said, shivering.

"I know, but it's quiet, and I want to be sure you hear every word. Are you listening?"

"Yes."

"Good." He backed away from her to drop down on one knee. "Rachel James, I love you, and I want to be part of your life, and Tommy's life. I want to be there for you and with you, each day, every day, for the rest of our lives. I want you to be my wife and the mother of my children. Marry me, Rachel," he said, drawing a ring from his pocket and slipping it onto her finger.

The white diamond glittered even in the patio lights. She stared down at the ring in shock and then at Cade. "You really mean it?" she breathed.

He rose and drew her into his arms. "More than I've ever meant anything." He caught her by the hips and pulled her more securely against him. "So is that a yes, Rachel? Are you going to marry me?"

She smiled up into his eyes, her heart so full that it bubbled over with love and hope and possibility. "Yes."

Epilogue

"Boss, looks like your missus is coming this way," Bill said with a nod.

Cade shoved his hat back on his head and looked up, and yes, indeed, she was, picking her way through the frost-covered pasture in his long brown suede coat. With the winter sun haloing her dark brown hair and the chill turning her cheeks pink and making her eyes shine, she looked both sexy and sweet, and he felt a rush of tenderness and a wave of protectiveness.

Rachel, his gorgeous girl, who was now his wife and the mother of his children, five-year-old Tommy and their sweet baby girl. And he'd always loved her, falling for her the moment she and her bike had collided into him, but that love was nothing compared to what he felt for her now.

"Hey," she said, reaching his side, her breath clouding, her eyes impossibly bright in her face.

His blood heated just looking at her. They'd made love early this morning before he'd left bed to get to work, but already he wanted her again. "What are you doing out here?"

"Madelyn's sleeping and Mrs. Brown is playing with Tommy so I thought I'd check on you."

"Check on me?"

"Make sure you weren't freezing to death out here. It's cold." She smiled, eyes dancing. "So I've brought you some hot coffee and love." She pulled a thermos out of one of the coat pockets and handed it to him, leaning in close to press a warm kiss to his cool lips. "Love you, Cade."

"Happy Valentine's Day, darlin'."

"Happy Valentine's Day, angel."

* * * * *

Hill Country Cupid

TANYA MICHAELS

Dear Reader,

As a writer, I always enjoy sharing my stories—but some projects are even more fun than others! I particularly love this Valentine collection because I'm being included with fantastic author Jane Porter and because I got to create a happy ending for Tess Fitzpatrick (one of my favorite secondary characters from my Hill Country Heroes series).

Ballet instructor Tess Fitzpatrick has never been able to resist meddling for a good cause. Single father Nick Calhoun devotes all his time to raising his six-year-old daughter, Bailey, and working on his family's ranch. He leaves the dating scene to his more outgoing brothers. But Tess knows just how much Bailey wants a mom and can't understand why more women haven't noticed how hot Nick is. When she decides to play matchmaker for the quiet cowboy, plans quickly go awry—especially when Nick realizes who he really wants as his Valentine.

Happy reading,

Tanya

My heartfelt thanks to all the wonderful readers who've let me know how much they enjoy the Hill Country Heroes series.

Chapter One

Although it had taken years—and repeated motherly lectures—for Tess Fitzpatrick to accept that she'd never be a prima ballerina, she had to admit she loved her life. She enjoyed her career as a dance instructor at the small studio, and she adored her students. Unlike people trapped in offices, watching their computer clocks and counting the minutes until they could go home, Tess was actually a bit disappointed to be ending the day's lessons. She was in no real hurry to go home and eat dinner by herself. But parents were waiting on the other side of the large observation window.

"Class dismissed," Tess told the roomful of bubbly kindergarten-aged girls. Several of them, including star pupil Josie Winchester, ran up to hug Tess before exiting into the lobby.

There was a flurry of activity as students exchanged tap shoes for sneakers and mothers bundled kids into coats to ward off the late January chill. Within moments, the crowd had dwindled to single mom Farrah Landon, texting while she waited for her daughter to emerge from the restroom, and six-year-old Bailey Calhoun, who sat in a folding metal chair with a glum expression.

Was the girl disappointed not to be chosen as a soloist? Several classes were combining to put on a special performance for parents during the studio's upcoming Valentine's party at the high school. Bailey had been in consideration for a part that ultimately went to Josie Winchester. It was a minor role in a brief presentation, but Tess understood the sting of being passed over for a chance at the spotlight.

She pulled a piece of chocolate from the jar she kept on the reception desk and went to Bailey's side. "Nice job today." She held out the candy. "I was impressed with how quickly you picked up the new combo steps."

"Thanks, Miss Tess." But neither the chocolate nor the compliment garnered a smile.

Tess ruffled the girl's dark hair. "I'm sure your dad will be here any minute."

Sure enough, the door swung open and in walked Nick Calhoun, Tess's favorite of the three Calhoun brothers. She was used to seeing him in the jeans and boots appropriate for outdoor work at his family's horse ranch, but today he wore a suit. He would have looked downright dashing if he hadn't seemed so ill at ease. As he walked, he tugged his tie loose.

"Daddy!" Bailey's face lit up like the annual Fourth of July fireworks.

Nick looked equally happy to see his daughter, affection obvious in his clear gray eyes. "Sorry I'm late, Bay." He was making a beeline toward them when he drew up short, belatedly noticing blond, willowy Farrah. "Hi."

"Hey, Rick," she said absently, not glancing up from her cell phone.

"Um, Nick. Nick Calhoun?"

That got her attention. "Oh, right! Your brother is Wyatt Calhoun."

He nodded.

"Tell him Farrah Landon said hi." She dropped her voice to a not-quite-whisper as her daughter returned to the lobby. "And remind him that I got divorced last year."

Platinum-haired mother and child exited the studio as

Nick waved halfheartedly in their wake. Then he whipped his head around, features flushed. Was he feeling guilty that he'd gotten sidetracked en route to his daughter or was he embarrassed to be caught watching Farrah?

He closed the distance between himself and Bailey, scooping her into his arms as if she weighed nothing, then apologized to Tess. "I had a meeting that took longer than expected."

"Not a problem." She grinned. "I'm guessing from the fancy duds it was important?"

"Discussing some plans for expansion with a loan officer. Dad should have sent Wyatt or Kevin. My brothers are better with...people." His self-deprecating tone made Tess wonder if the loan officer was a woman. Nick darted a glance over his shoulder, in the direction Farrah and her daughter had gone, and sighed. Then he shook his head, smiling once again at his daughter. "You hungry?"

"Starving!"

"Guess we'd better track you down some dinner before you waste away to nothing," he teased.

They were headed for the door when Bailey suddenly swiveled around. "Miss Tess? Did I really do good today?"

"Didn't I say so?" Tess winked at the little girl. "I never say anything I don't mean."

Once the studio was empty, Tess used the time to finalize the choreography for the Valentine's performance. As she locked up for the night, she recalled Nick's wistful expression. No secret who he wanted for his valentine. But Farrah had seemed oblivious. It didn't look as if Nick had a shot— although this *was* the season for romance. Maybe Cupid would decide to intervene on his behalf.

TESS SILENTLY CHANTED positive thoughts as she entered the bridal boutique Saturday morning. *I am excited for my friend. I am happy for my friend.* After all, it had been Tess who encouraged Lorelei Keller to get romantically involved with Sam Travis in the first place. Tess was thrilled Sam and Lorelei were getting married during Frederick-Fest, the weeklong event that had helped bring them together last spring. So what if their March wedding meant Tess would be wearing her third bridesmaid dress in two years? Prior to this, she'd been in the bridal party for her elegant, swanlike sister, Regina, as well as newly married Heather Winchester.

"Tess! You're here!" Lorelei, not typically a hugger, rushed forward to embrace her. Then she drew back, abashed. "Sorry, didn't mean to tackle you."

"No problem. It's nice to feel so welcome," Tess quipped.

"I couldn't do this without you! You'd think such a small wedding would be easier to manage." Since neither bride nor groom had much family, the ceremony would be an intimate affair in the heart of town with Tess as maid of honor and an old rodeo buddy of Sam's as best man. The reception afterward would be held at the B and B Lorelei and Sam ran together.

Lorelei's dark eyes shimmered with unshed tears. "Usually, I'm great with details, but I'm turning into an emotional basket case. I miss Mom."

The one-year anniversary of Wanda Keller's death was only a couple of weeks away; as much as Tess's own family drove her nuts, she couldn't imagine getting married without either of her parents being alive to see it. "Wanda would have been so happy for you," Tess said. "You know how she adored Sam."

Lorelei nodded. "We've been trying to decide how to honor her during the ceremony. One of her friends suggested I wear Mom's 'lucky pig' jewelry, but I'm not sold on the idea."

Tess chuckled at the mental image of whimsical pigs

paired with her friend's simple strapless gown. "Don't worry, you still have a month to brainstorm."

The two women joined the boutique manager, who led them to luxurious changing rooms for their fittings. Of all the bridesmaid dresses Tess had worn so far, the deep red gown Lorelei had picked was her favorite. There was something about the cut that made Tess feel taller (she'd always been dwarfed by her lithe mother and sister) and the cleavage revealed by the scooped neckline was flattering. She looked curvy rather than chubby. Tess wasn't exactly overweight— not by more than five or ten pounds—but she was by far the most solidly built of the Fitzpatrick women.

Slender Lorelei was even taller than Tess's sister. Tess dreaded the wedding photos of the bride and maid of honor alone. *Vera Wang Meets Abbott and Costello.* Maybe Tess could lose a few pounds before the ceremony. And wear very high heels.

Through the partition separating them, she called to Lorelei, "You have a great eye for color." Conventional wisdom suggested the red might clash with Tess's hair, but the color was so dark it somehow toned down her curls, making them appear more burnished-gold than orange. "This dress is terrific."

A few minutes later, Tess breathed, "I stand corrected. *That* dress is terrific." Lorelei stood on a dais while the seamstress checked her hem. The bride-to-be looked phenomenal, her dark hair and eyes a dramatic contrast to the beaded white dress. "Sam is one lucky guy."

Lorelei grinned wryly. "Yeah, if you overlook the fact that he's saddling himself with an increasingly unstable woman and her demon cat." There had been jokes about putting a little pouch around Oberon's feline neck and letting him be the ring bearer, but Sam had insisted the temperamental pet would get revenge.

After they'd changed back into their regular clothes, Tess invited her friend to lunch. "I'm craving The Twisted Jalapeño. Wanna join me?"

"I never pass up an opportunity to eat Grace's food! And the menu's gotten even more amazing since she partnered with that hunky co-owner. Should I follow you, or do you want to ride together?"

They decided it would be more fun to go in the same car and come back for Lorelei's. As Tess drove, they discussed business at the ballet studio, recent movies and Valentine's Day being only a few weeks away. Since their romantic B and B was a popular destination for lovers, Lorelei and Sam would be working over the holiday but planned to make up the time over their honeymoon. For her part, Tess figured she'd stick with the tradition of attending the big town Valentine dance.

Discussing the romantic holiday made Tess think of Nick and his yearning expression yesterday evening. "Hey, Lor, wouldn't you say Nick Calhoun is attractive?"

Lorelei looked at her blankly from the passenger seat. "Who?"

"I forgot, the only man you ever notice is the one you're engaged to," Tess teased. "He's the youngest of the three Calhoun brothers. You know, the family who owns the Galloping C Ranch?"

"Oh, right. Sam's done some work for them." Lorelei straightened in her seat. "Wait, are you asking because *you're* attracted to Nick? Even though we're keeping the guest list small, you can still bring a 'plus one' to the wedding."

"I'm not asking for me. I just meant…in general." If gorgeous Lorelei saw his appeal, perhaps it wouldn't be far-fetched that Farrah could appreciate him, too.

"'In general?'" Lorelei sounded baffled. But she pursed her lips and considered the question.

"He's the brother with darker hair," Tess supplied helpfully. Wyatt and Kevin both had sandy-brown hair, just a few shades past blond. The color of Nick's hair was richer, as dark as undiluted coffee.

"I think I remember Nick now. He's the short one, right?"

"He's six feet! Maybe he's not as tall as his brothers, but we can't all be Amazons." Tess stopped, chagrined by how defensive she sounded. "Sorry. Personal hot button."

People rarely realized how tall Nick was because he was so often in the company of his brothers and father. Plus, he'd grown up with a tendency to shrink into himself when embarrassed. Back in elementary school, where he'd only been a grade ahead of Tess, he'd slouched when other kids made fun of his stutter.

But he'd grown into perfect articulation and a deep voice with a pleasant hint of raspiness. What Nick needed—and Farrah, too, for that matter—was a wake-up call. The six-foot cowboy bore no resemblance to the awkward, stammering boy he'd once been.

Tess drummed her fingers on the steering wheel. All he needed was a blast of confidence. And possibly a haircut.

"Uh-oh," Lorelei said suddenly.

Tess blinked. "What? What is it?"

"You have That Look. You're planning on interfering with some unsuspecting citizen's life, aren't you? That's the same look you got when you decided enough was enough and gave Asha Macpherson a piece of your mind about the way she talks to her daughter in public."

"Someone needed to! All that 'constructive criticism' was humiliating the hell out of Juliet. Far as I can tell, my chat worked. No one's seen Juliet break down and cry lately. They were at the movies last Saturday and looked like they were having a very nice mother-daughter outing."

"And of course," Lorelei continued, "you used to get that

same gleam in your eye when you harangued me about seducing Sam."

"Which, you must admit, worked out pretty well," Tess said with a grin.

"No complaints here. Actually, I admire your instincts. I'm great at understanding numbers, but your gift is people."

One could only hope Nick would be as admiring of Tess's gift. Because her friend was right—Tess had officially decided to interfere.

Chapter Two

Though it was barely noon, Nick felt as if he'd already put in a full day's work. Since his mom had taken Bailey to visit relatives in San Antonio, he was making the most of a free Saturday. He and ranch hand Tim Mullins were trying to catch up on routine maintenance before the busy spring season. Now they could cross "Replace cracked tractor seat" off the to-do list.

Handing the wrench back to Tim, a Texas A&M graduate the Calhouns had hired two years ago, Nick got to his feet. He dusted his hands across his faded jeans. "Everything else I plan to accomplish requires a trip into town for supplies. Want to come with me, maybe grab some lunch after I clean up?"

Tim's grin flashed white against his dark skin. "See, *that's* what you need to do."

"What the hell are you talking about?"

"You, casually inviting someone to join you for a meal. And by someone, I mean Farrah Landon."

"I rescind the invitation," Nick grumbled. "I'll just run to town by myself."

Tim fell into step with him, undeterred. "I realize your ex was before my time—maybe if I'd met her, I'd get why you're still hung up—but don't you think it's time to move on?"

"You think I still have feelings for Marla?" Nick asked in

disbelief. His wife had left him four years ago for a wealthy real-estate developer in Galveston. She rarely crossed Nick's mind unless Bailey mentioned her.

"Um...I may have heard it somewhere."

Mom. It was the responsibility of Nick's dad to worry about the horses and land; it was the responsibility of Erin Calhoun to fret over their sons. She'd always been extraprotective of her youngest.

"Trust me, Marla is ancient history," Nick said. "I'm better off without her."

"So why don't you date? In all the time I've known you, I can count on one hand—"

"I'm a single dad," Nick interrupted, feeling a little guilty for playing the Bailey card. It was true she kept him busy and also true that his being a father added pressure to potential relationships. But there were other issues, too. Half the women in his social circle had known him as a stuttering adolescent, the other half were busy drooling over his brothers. The easiest time he'd ever had talking to members of the opposite sex had been away at college, where he'd met Marla.

"Doesn't Farrah have a kid?" Tim countered.

"Two," Nick admitted. "One Bay's age and one a few years older."

"Then she'd probably consider your parenting experience a good thing. C'mon, I've noticed you noticing her."

"Didn't anyone ever tell you harassing your boss about his personal life is bad for job security?"

"All right, all right. I'll drop it." Tim relented. "For now."

"SPEAK OF THE DEVIL." Lorelei paused, her chip halfway to the salsa verde. "You know that guy you were telling me about?"

"Nick?" Tess asked.

"Isn't that him?" Lorelei gestured with her chin toward the hostess podium. "Just walking in now?"

Tess glanced over her shoulder to see Nick Calhoun, once again in his customary jeans, with a handsome guy who looked as if he could be actor Morris Chestnut's younger brother.

"Huh." Lorelei swung her gaze back to Tess, her expression surprised. "I never really paid attention before, but Nick *is* good-looking. Are you sure he even needs help getting a valentine?"

"You should know better than anyone that sometimes people could use a nudge in the right direction."

"And you are going to be that nudge."

Tess gave her a beatific smile. "Precisely." She hoped the hostess would pass their way while leading the men to a table, but the trio went toward the opposite side of the restaurant. Moments later, a waitress brought Tess and Lorelei their food.

At the end of the meal, when Lorelei excused herself to the ladies' room, Tess decided it was time to act. Her short trip across the restaurant was lengthened by the number of people who called out greetings and wanted to chat with her. Tess had lived here her entire life and had been just as outgoing a child as she was an adult. She knew almost everyone, though she couldn't recall the name of Nick's lunch companion.

The man gave her a warm smile as she approached. "Well, hello."

"Hi," Tess said. "I don't believe we've met."

Nick made the introductions. "Tim Mullins, Tess Fitzpatrick. Tim's our most recent hire at the Galloping C, but he lives out closer to Luckenbach. Tess is Bailey's dance teacher. Bay adores her."

"The feeling's mutual," Tess said fondly. "I don't mean to interrupt y'all's lunch, but could I steal Nick for a second?"

"Steal away," Tim said approvingly. "In fact, I just realized I left my cell phone in the truck. I should get it. In case anyone, um, tries to reach me." With that, he was out of his chair in one fluid movement and headed for the exit.

Tess blinked. "He's certainly accommodating."

"He's a lot of things." Nick sounded exasperated. He shook it off, returning his gaze to her as she slid into Tim's vacated seat. "What's up? Is there something we need to discuss about Bailey? I really am sorry I was late getting her last night. Was she worried I forgot about her?"

"Bailey is a joy to have in class and if she was bothered by your tardiness, she forgave you the minute you came through the door. I actually wanted to discuss…you."

He leaned back in his chair, looking confused. "Me? Are you recruiting parent volunteers for the Valentine party? Decorations and homemade cookies aren't really—"

"Nick, we've known each other a long time, right?" Not that they were close, but they'd gone to school together, they saw each other on a weekly basis and they always stopped to exchange pleasantries when they encountered each other in town.

"Sure."

"Then I hope you'll forgive me for being blunt." Tess had realized early in life that she was never going to be the refined, demure Fitzpatrick sister and had embraced her brashness. "I couldn't help notice that when you ran into Farrah yesterday—"

"Not you, too!" Nick groaned. "I've been getting this from Tim all morning. Apparently I have the world's worst poker face."

"Think of it as being expressive and sincere," Tess suggested. "Qualities women like. In fact, I think any woman would be lucky to go out with you."

"Thanks, but I'm not sure past experience bears out that opinion."

"Those experiences are behind you, Nick. It's a brandnew day! Consider me your guardian angel. Your fairy godmother. Or, not to put too fine a point on it, your muchneeded swift kick in the ass."

Chapter Three

"I beg your pardon?" Nick couldn't quite wrap his mind around what Tess was saying. She'd always struck him as boisterous, possibly unpredictable, but never mentally unstable. Until now. Normal people didn't go around offering to be winged, wand-toting guardians for casual acquaintances. She was right that they'd known each other for years, but he couldn't recall their ever having such a personal conversation. "What brought this on? Did you lose a bet or something?" *I swear to God, if my brothers put her up to this...*

"It's almost Valentine's Day. I'm getting in touch with my inner Cupid. Besides, anyone in town can tell you I'm incapable of minding my own business."

"Are *you* seeing anyone? I was under the impression you're single."

Her pale cheeks flushed rose. "Not relevant."

"Why not play Cupid for yourself?"

She surprised him with a sassy grin, already recovered from her nanosecond of embarrassment. "That's not how it works, genius. Cupid doesn't shoot himself in the butt with his own arrows. Or, in my case, her arrows. However, if there was someone I was seriously interested in, you can bet I wouldn't be too shy to let him know."

"Fair point. You are clearly not the shy type."

"Whereas *you*... You just need a few pointers, a bit of confidence, some practice."

He was almost afraid to ask what kind of practice. "Tess, this is, uh, nice of you." Damned odd, yet nice in a misguided sort of way. "It's not necessary, though. I admit, I find Farrah attractive. I always have." He'd had a huge crush on her for most of high school. He hadn't thought about her much while away at college, but now that they were both single again... "If a relationship's meant to be between us, shouldn't it happen naturally?"

She made a dismissive *pffft* sound. "That's ridiculous. Everything in life that's worth anything takes work."

Where the heck was Tim? As long as the man was taking, he could have walked all the way back to the ranch for his cell phone. Nick glanced around, hoping for an excuse to end this conversation quickly without being rude. He spotted the ranch hand at the bar, chatting amiably with the bartender. *Traitor.*

"Take my dancing," Tess continued blithely. "Was I born with some natural aptitude and a love for ballet? You betcha. But it still required hours and hours of practice and fine-tuning. And what about the Galloping C? When it comes to breeding the horses you sell, are you telling me you just turn them loose in the pasture and hope for the best?"

He stared, dumbfounded by her comparison. "That's, uh, not exactly..."

"Right. Of course not." She waved a hand. "I wasn't saying you and Farrah are like horses. Look, Nick, I know I've caught you off guard. You don't have to give me an answer right now. But my offer stands. When you decide to take me up on it, call me."

THE TINY TWO-BEDROOM house on the edge of the Galloping C property was nearly identical to the bungalows the Calhouns rented to guests. What set Nick's place apart, what truly made it home for him, were the accumulated pictures and mementos of Bailey's first six years and the frequent ring of her laughter echoing through the rooms.

Sunday evening found him sitting cross-legged on the floor of his daughter's bedroom, pretending to sip from a plastic teacup. To his left, Bailey's favorite teddy bear perched in one of the dainty chairs that matched the plastic table.

"How's your tea?" he asked his daughter. She brewed the best imaginary pot this side of the Rio Grande.

"Oh, no!" She clutched a hand to her throat. "Mine wasn't tea. It was *potion*."

He wasn't sure if she meant the magical variety or if she'd mistaken the word for *poison,* so he simply waited, ever-ready to play along.

"The ninjas must be trying to get me again!" She reached beneath the small table to pull out a long cardboard tube that had once held a roll of paper towels. "Here's your sword, Daddy! Fight off those ninjas."

"Aye, aye, Captain." He wasn't sure the naval terminology was strictly logical for a ninja-infested tea party, but his daughter beamed encouragingly, adopting the pirate theme and running with it.

"If you capture all the ninjas, Teddy can make them walk the plank."

"We have a plank?" he inquired. "Since when?"

Bailey hopped onto her bed, extending a pillow over the floor. "This is the plank. But now…everything is…" She gurgled dramatically. "Going black." She fell straight backward, shooting her legs up into the air.

Nick went to her side and dropped a kiss on her forehead. "I am so glad you're my daughter. I bet other little girls' tea parties aren't half as exciting."

"I'm glad you're my daddy." She hugged him. "Because you love me *so much* you even let me stay up late."

"Nice try, Bay, but you have school tomorrow. Time to brush your teeth."

She huffed out her breath in disappointment and trudged toward the bathroom. His strong-willed, highly inventive daughter reminded him of Tess Fitzpatrick and her out-of-the-blue proposal yesterday. It was easy to imagine Bailey growing up to be like the pretty dance teacher, outrageous enough to accost people with unsolicited advice.

Outrageous, but good-hearted.

When he'd been a kid, often too embarrassed to speak to anyone, Tess would say hi to him on the playground, asking if he wanted to swing with her or play catch. She'd been happy to babble and monopolize conversation, so he had little reason to worry about his own articulation.

But was he grateful enough for past kindnesses to let her play matchmaker? What exactly was she envisioning—that she'd stand off to the side texting him suggested dialogue like some kind of modern-day Cyrano? He shuddered.

He didn't want any games or forced awkwardness. And if that meant Farrah never saw him as anything other than Wyatt Calhoun's younger brother... His lip curled. Actually, the idea of Farrah never seeing him for himself sucked.

By the time Bailey returned to the room, she'd regained the bounce in her step.

"Am I still the best daddy even though I'm making you go to bed?" Nick teased.

She nodded, yawning. "I have the best daddy. But Cousin Amber has the best mommy. I want a mommy, too."

"You have a mother, Bay. And she loves you very much." The words were like sawdust in his mouth. Would it be so difficult for Marla to call her daughter once in a while? Maybe send a freaking card? "She just doesn't live here."

The gray eyes Bailey had inherited from him took on a steely determination. "Suzie in my class has two moms. Her old mom moved away, but then her dad got married. Suzie got to carry flowers in the wedding and wear a dress like a princess. Now she has a new mom who lives at her house. Why don't you do that?"

So many reasons, kid. "It's getting late." He gave a melo-dramatically exaggerated yawn that made her giggle. "How about we discuss this in the morning?"

Nick made sure her night-light was turned on, said bed-time prayer with her, then wandered back to the kitchen. Bailey had come home from dance class Friday with the February newsletter, and he'd stuck it to the refrigerator with a magnet. As always, Tess had included a note at the bottom with her cell number, urging parents to phone her if they ever had any questions or concerns. He scowled at the digits printed on the paper. Was he really considering calling her?

What about the philosophy of relationships developing naturally? The idea that he'd meet a woman someday and that events would unfold artlessly sounded good. But that strategy had gotten him nowhere in the past four years. He pulled the newsletter off the fridge and sighed.

Time to consider a new strategy.

Chapter Four

Standing in the middle of his kitchen, Nick dialed quickly, knowing that if he hesitated, he'd talk himself out of this.

"Hello?" Tess caught him off guard by answering midway through the first ring. A person practically had to be psychic to answer the phone that fast.

"Oh. Hi. This is Nick." Not sure how to proceed, he added, "Calhoun."

She chuckled softly. "I knew which Nick."

"Well, it *is* a pretty common name."

"True. But you're the only Nick I was waiting to hear from."

"You were really that confident I'd call?" Because he was still surprised by his own actions.

"I have the innate ability to wear people down. But this is actually sooner than I anticipated. I thought it would require further stalking."

Her completely unrepentant tone tugged a half grin from him. However unorthodox Tess might be, she was likable.

"So expecting my call wasn't why you pounced on the phone, then?"

"No, that was a maid-of-honor thing," Tess said. "Lorelei and I have been playing phone tag all night. I'd barely hung up from leaving her a voice mail when it rang again. I assumed it was her. I'm glad it's you."

"That makes one of us," he grumbled. Aware of how ungrateful he sounded, he added, "It's embarrassing to ask for help in this area."

"You didn't ask, I offered."

"Even worse." He reached into the fridge and pulled out a beer. But instead of opening the can, he held it to his temple. He'd been fighting a headache since his daughter's announcement that Suzie had a new mommy. "That means it was obvious that I *needed* help. I must be missing some Calhoun gene. My brothers have never asked anyone for dating advice."

"Last I checked, neither of your brothers is in a happy, stable relationship, either."

Huh. He hadn't really thought of it that way, but she was right. Kevin drifted aimlessly from one woman to the next while Wyatt seemed stuck in a destructive on-again, off-again cycle with a professional barrel racer.

"What changed your mind?" Tess prompted.

"My kid. I was hoping, since we're surrounded by family, including my mom, who bakes birthday cakes and braids hair for ballet recitals, that Bailey didn't feel like there was a big mother-shaped hole in her life. But I was kidding myself. She wants me to remarry. There was talk of being a flower girl and wearing a fancy dress." *Thanks a lot, Suzie, you troublemaker.*

"Not that I would propose to anyone on the whim of a six-year-old," he added wryly. "But maybe I should be more open to possibilities."

"Possibilities like Farrah Landon?" she said knowingly.

He laughed. "That's aiming pretty high. I decided at fourteen she was my dream girl—and haven't managed to speak to her coherently since." He was surprised to have admitted that. But what could he possibly say to Tess to make the situation any more awkward than it already was? Which, in a way, was liberating.

"Ironic that Bay wants a mom," he said. "The cliché is every girl wants a pony—"

"Not every little girl!"

"—and I could give her a herd of ponies. A mom, on the other hand..." He belatedly registered her adamant tone. "You don't like horses?"

"I like them just fine. From a distance."

"I didn't think anything intimidated the Brash and Fearless Tess Fitzpatrick."

"It's not like I'm phobic or anything," she said, trying too hard to sound casual about it. "I just don't have much practice on horseback."

"How 'bout I make you a deal? You step outside *your* comfort zone and go riding with me, and I'll step outside mine and accept your help when it comes to the ladies. It'll be character-building for both of us."

A long moment passed before she grudgingly agreed. "Fine. But only because you really need my help."

TESS WAS ABOUT TO ACCEPT Tim's offer to walk her to the barn when Kevin, the middle Calhoun brother, stepped out of the trailer that served as a small administrative office.

"I'll take her." Kevin's mouth curved into the automatic grin he gave all women, and he treated her to a lingering once-over that made her skin itch. She was tempted to kick him in the shin with one of her not-quite-broken-in boots. "It'll give Contessa and me a chance to catch up on old times."

Instead of glaring at the use of her hated full name, Tess smiled sweetly. "Which old times? The month when you tried unsuccessfully to get my sister to go out with you or when you never called my cousin again after three dates? She had some *really* interesting things to say about you."

Kevin's self-assured expression faltered. "You know what? I forgot I promised to help Dad this afternoon. I guess Tim should show you the way after all."

"Well, shoot." Tess's mock disappointment earned a stifled guffaw from Tim.

"So what brings you here in the middle of a Tuesday?" the ranch hand asked as they started down a smooth dirt path. "I know Nick's expecting you, but he was…sort of weird about it."

"Ha! Nick's the most normal of the bunch. *That* one is weird." Tess jerked a thumb over her shoulder, back where they'd left Kevin. It eluded her how anyone could think the smarmy man was more attractive than Nick. "Does he really expect women to fall at his feet? Any female who's lived around here more than a month knows what an unreliable hound he is. The only ones who think his full-court press is genuine are the tourists." Poor things. Maybe Tess should talk to the city council about posting warnings.

Tim peered at her. "Miss Fitzpatrick, did you just duck my question?"

"About why I'm here? Nick's doing me a favor. I'm uncomfortable around horses, and he offered to help." More like *blackmailed,* but she could respect that.

"Ah. Well, here we are."

In the shade of the barn, the crispness of the air became downright frosty. Nick emerged from the barn into the sunshine, smiling his welcome.

"Good to see you, Tess. Glad you didn't change your mind."

"I considered it, but I think it's so important for people to leave their comfort zones and take some risks. Don't you?"

He smirked at her. "Maybe I should have saddled a more spirited ride for you than Ambling Aimee."

"Oh, I'm sure Aimee will be just fine." She prided herself on not sounding shaky as she thanked Tim and bade him goodbye.

He tipped his weathered straw hat. "Good luck, ma'am."

Once she and Nick were alone, she scolded him for the gleam in his silvery eyes. "It's not chivalrous to look delighted by my terror."

"Oh, please," he retorted skeptically. "I know you're apprehensive, but 'terror'? How scared of horses can you be? You were born and raised in Texas."

"Believe it or not, being an accomplished equestrienne isn't technically a requirement to live here."

"But…hell, Bailey's been riding since she was practically a toddler."

"I don't suppose she has a pony I could borrow?" On second thought, Tess might break it. When she'd pulled on her old pair of jeans that morning, she'd been dismayed they fit so snugly.

Nick led her inside the barn. The scents of leather and hay would have been pleasant if they weren't also accompanied by the earthier—and more foreboding—smell of horses. Whinnies and snorts came from the shadowed recesses of the stalls. "Did something happen to make you scared of horses?" he asked sympathetically. "Bad fall? One of them kick you?"

She grimaced. "No, but thanks for highlighting those possibilities. The worst summer of my adolescence was spent at a camp I didn't want to attend in the first place. The counselors were determined to help me love horses, but each stab at riding went worse than the last."

At the time, it had felt as though all the other campers were reveling in her humiliation. "The final straw was a mean-spirited devil who deemed me unworthy as soon as I got in the saddle. He tried for fifteen minutes to unseat me. After a dead run at a low branch, I decided decapitation wasn't worth the activity points I could earn for my cabin. That was my last time on horseback."

Nick clucked his tongue. "Haven't you heard the saying about getting back in the saddle? You have to try again."

"Said the pot to the kettle. It's been what, four years since your divorce?" She softened her observation with a cajoling smile. "Womankind needs you. There has to be an alternative to guys like your obnoxious brother. He's lucky I didn't kick him."

His eyes narrowed. "Tell me Kevin did not hit on you."

"Worse, he called me *Contessa*. Everyone knows I hate my full name."

"You shouldn't. It's unique, which certainly fits you. And isn't *contessa* nobility or royalty somewhere? That fits, too. You have subjects who love you—well, students—and an innate talent for telling people what to do."

"I'd be annoyed that you just called me bossy except it's totally true."

"Enough stalling." He tugged lightly on her hand. "C'mon, Contessa. It's my turn to give the orders now."

AFTER LAUGHING AT TESS'S refusal to feed the horse a carrot— the pale gold beast might be gentle natured, but she had *huge* teeth—Nick helped her onto the mare and had her practice in the ring they used for children's birthday parties. Unlike the monster she'd previously ridden, the one who'd tried to behead her, Ambling Aimee accepted Tess with an air of melancholy resignation. *Not unlike my mother, actually.*

Nick excused himself to saddle his own horse so they could ride out in the pasture. Tess had reminded him that this had to be a brief ride—she had a dance class to teach later. He returned quickly, leading a dark red horse whose black saddle matched its mane and tail.

"This is North Star. She's often the lead horse on our trail rides. If you nodded off and slept for the next twenty minutes, Aimee would still follow along with no problem. You don't have to worry about her going rogue." He opened the gate to the ring, clucking his tongue at Aimee. "Ready to really stretch your legs, girl?"

Tess made a concerted effort not to tighten her grip on the reins. Acres and acres of pastureland spread out beneath the blue sky. Lots of space for something to go wrong.

Nick met her gaze. "You're doing great."

"So are you. You say your brothers are the naturals when it comes to talking to women, but you've been charming and funny and patient." She seized the chance to think about something other than how far away the ground looked. "Show Farrah this side of you, and she'll be putty in your hands."

He flushed. "Trying to start a conversation with her is a lot different than this."

Right. Because Tess was more the nonintimidating buddy type than the leggy femme fatale.

She had a sudden flash to her freshman year in high school, to a crush on an older member of the debate team. A crush she'd foolishly believed to be mutual. It hadn't been until he'd finally worked up the nerve to ask her sister to prom that Tess realized why he'd been finding so many excuses to spend time at the Fitzpatrick house.

After Regina shot him down, he and Tess had gone together, as friends. "This will probably be more fun anyway," he'd said as they left her house on prom night. "You're not someone a guy has to worry about impressing." Prom made many young ladies in their glamorous dresses feel like princesses for the evening—Cinderella at the ball. For Tess, it had been like a jarring realization that she was actually the short, squat stepsister. She flinched at the memory, apparently jerking on the reins because Aimee came to an obedient, if unexpected, halt.

"Everything okay?" Nick asked.

"Sure. We're, uh, just waiting for you."

He pulled himself up into the saddle with such easy grace that Tess stared. She'd worked for countless hours to cultivate poise on stage; Nick's rugged elegance was simply who he was.

"My family's owned this ranch my entire life," Nick said as their horses fell in step. "We get tourists, especially in the spring and summer, and I'm used to dealing with them. If I'm saddling a horse for someone, I know how to make small talk. When I'm on the trail, I can discuss the plants in bloom or facts about livestock. None of that's the same as asking a woman out."

A moment later, he added, "It's not even the asking I mind, really."

"Is it fear they'll say no?" Seeing his strong profile beneath the brim of his hat, the way he effortlessly commanded a thousand-pound animal, she couldn't imagine what idiot woman would refuse him.

"Sometimes it's worse when they say yes. I have had a few dates in the last couple of years, you know. Nothing ruins a perfectly good dinner like awkward conversation. Or the awkward lack thereof. With one girl, I skipped the dinner fiasco entirely and just took her to the movies." He brightened. "That night ended pretty well."

Tess did not want details. "You can't base a relationship on just movies and…other activities that don't require talking. Eventually you'd have to speak to her. All you need is practice. You've been riding horses your whole life, right?" At his prompt nod, she continued, "But your parents didn't send you off at a full gallop your first time out of the gate. We just need to start small. And maybe…"

"What?"

She hesitated. On the drive over here, she'd planned to ask him how he'd feel about a slight change in image. A haircut, some new shirts—just a few minor tweaks that might help Farrah see him in a different light. But Tess was abruptly reluctant. He looked pretty damn good already.

"Tess?"

"I, uh…" She swallowed. "Sorry. Lost my train of thought."

His expression turned sympathetic. "Nerves? We can turn back to the barn if you want."

"What? Oh, no. Aimee and I are doing just fine." Tess had momentarily forgotten she was even on horseback. She'd been too caught up in Nick. *You mean, caught up in how to help him.* That's why she was here, after all. "Do you see many movies? If this were a romantic comedy, we'd be coming up on a makeover sequence, complete with musical montage."

"Makeover?" He eyed her suspiciously. "The movies I like have shoot-outs, not manicures."

"Which would be helpful if you wanted to kill a guy at high noon. Not so helpful in winning you a valentine. Don't worry, I'm not talking about a full-on makeover. No one's suggesting highlights or a spray tan—"

"I should hope the hell not!"

"But a haircut couldn't hurt, perhaps some new clothes. All of which we can get at a mall. Know what else is at the mall?"

"A bunch of overpriced stuff I don't need?"

"Women. Female salesclerks, stylists, shoppers. Lots of chances for you to practice nonranching small talk."

"Sounds like a blast," he said grimly.

"There's a teacher planning day at the end of the week—my students are all excited about a day off school. We can take Bailey and make an outing of it, hit the food court for lunch, let her ride the big merry-go-round. How bad could it be, a full day of shopping and my shoving you into constant conversation with total strangers?"

"This is payback for making you get on a horse, isn't it?"

No, that was just an added bonus. She gave him a sunny smile. "Why, Mr. Calhoun, I hope you don't think I'm vindictive."

He chuckled. "What I think is, it would be a mistake to ever underestimate you."

That cinched it—he was not only the good-looking Calhoun brother, he was the smart one, too.

Chapter Five

Tess pushed away her empty salad bowl and resisted the urge to steal one of Nick's heavenly-smelling French fries. A few yards away, Bailey waited her turn to go down the spiral slide that dominated the indoor playground. Nick had made the mistake of telling her she could play as soon as she'd finished her food; she'd inhaled her chicken nuggets and macaroni so quickly it was a wonder she hadn't choked.

Now that the two adults were alone, Tess could dispense advice freely. It had seemed wrong to give Nick tips on picking up women in front of his six-year-old. "I know I said you need practice talking to women, but it's not all about what you say. Being a good listener is a *very* sexy trait. And a smile can be just as effective as words. Especially a smile like yours."

He tilted his head, regarding her with a mixture of chagrin and amusement. "I appreciate your trying to inspire confidence, but you don't have to resort to flattery."

"I never say anything I don't mean!" She fixed him with a reproving look. "You know better than that."

He thought she'd been exaggerating the truth to bolster him? The man must not own a mirror. He wasn't like his brother Kevin, a sly grin always at the ready, but Nick's smiles were infinitely more appealing. Ever since Nick and Bailey had picked her up at her house that morning, Tess had watched him joke with his daughter, particularly enjoying the way his eyes gleamed silver when he laughed.

Nick pressed the heel of his hand to his forehead. "You want me to chat up a bunch of strangers when I can't even talk to *you* without putting my foot in my mouth?"

"People say things that come out wrong all the time. Just say you're sorry and move on."

"That easy, huh?"

"Yep, that easy." Honesty compelled her to add, "More or less."

IF NICK WAS AMBIVALENT about entering the expensive-looking salon on the second floor of the mall, his daughter was outright hostile.

"Why do I hafta get my bangs cut?" she asked, thrusting her lower lip out so far it was in a different zip code than the rest of her face.

"Because I miss seeing your pretty eyes," Nick said, signing both their names on the waiting list. "I've forgotten what you look like. If your bangs get any longer, you're gonna start walking into walls."

From behind the wild fringe that hung halfway to her nose, Bailey glared. At least, that's the impression he got. But she kept any further complaints to herself, leaving his side to peruse a children's magazine rack.

Nick dropped into the chair next to Tess, imitating his daughter's melodramatic whine. "Do I *hafta* get my hair cut? It's not fairrr."

Giggling, Tess shoved his shoulder. "Cowboy up. Set a good example for your kid." A moment later, she bit her lip. "You won't let them cut too much, though, will you?"

"I thought the point was to make me less shaggy."

"Yeah, but… You look good exactly as you are. It's just that, after people have known each other a long time, sometimes it takes kind of a lightbulb moment to get them to think of each other differently. You're not a stammering fourteen-year-old kid anymore. You only need enough of a change to make Farrah do a double take, to really *see* you."

It sounded good in theory, but given Farrah's seeming disinterest when he'd said hi to her at the studio last Friday, earning a double take might require something drastic. Like a mohawk. Or an Afro. "How do you think I'd look with a buzz cut?"

"Don't even joke about that!" Tess lifted a hand, sifting her fingers through his hair. It felt far better than it should. His scalp tingled beneath her touch, and he had the urge to lean closer.

"Miss Tess, can you help me?" Bay crawled into her ballet teacher's lap. "I'm looking for hidden pictures."

"Then you're in luck," Tess said. "Because I excel at finding those. It's one of my five-hundred-and-thirteen talents."

Bailey's eyes widened. "That's a lot. What are the other five hundred and…" She trailed off, her lips moving silently as she calculated. "Twelve? Is one of them fighting ninjas? Daddy and I do that at our tea parties. Maybe you could help us."

The two females were discussing what style hat one wore to a formal gathering that included kung-fu combat when a woman with purple hair called Nick's name. "Mr. Calhoun?"

Tess slid Bailey to Nick's now-unoccupied chair and walked toward the stylist, giving cheerful instructions.

The woman nodded. "Got it. Don't worry, your husband is in good hands with me. He'll look even hotter when I'm through."

Tess's face flushed. "Oh, no, we're not… He isn't…"

"Sorry." The stylist ducked her magenta-tinged head. "I saw the three of you sitting together and assumed… My bad."

Nick followed her to a chair at the back of the salon, thinking that he could understand her error. Anyone who'd watched Tess with Bailey today could easily conclude the two were mother and daughter. They'd been holding hands through the mall, playing guessing games and singing non-

sensical songs. On the isolated occasions Tess had repri-
manded the little girl for something, Bailey had immediately
corrected her behavior. They didn't look alike physically,
but Bay didn't much resemble Marla, either, having inherited Nick's coloring.

Still, Tess and Bailey shared some sort of indefinable
inner light, the same enthusiastic natures. Nick's parents
were good people; they'd tried their best to do right by their
sons but there'd never been a sense of playfulness in his
home. Until Bailey was born, the closest anyone in the family had come to a sense of humor was Kevin, but his "wit"
centered far too much on his supposed prowess with women.
There were few things Nick enjoyed more than laughing with
his daughter. Before today, he hadn't given much thought to
how rarely he laughed with other adults.

The stylist dampened his hair with a spray bottle. "So if
you two aren't married, are you at least dating? Usually my
instincts about couples are spot-on."

"Sorry to end your streak, but no."

"Platonic acquaintances don't get that intense about each
other's haircuts. And did you see how she blushed? She likes
you."

*Yeah, she's so crazy about me that she's going out of her
way to throw me at other women.* Nick returned the stylist's
smile in the mirror but didn't bother responding.

What would Tess see in him? He was a horse-raising cowboy who occasionally found it difficult to articulate consecutive sentences; he had little time to date and the only dance
performance he'd been to in his entire life was Bailey's recital last spring. Tess's two favorite things in life seemed to
be ballet and conversation, and she wasn't fond of horses.
All they had in common were ancient playground history
and affection for his daughter. Tess Fitzpatrick was exactly
what she'd always been, an outspoken yet supportive friend.

Nothing more.

TESS STOPPED JUST INSIDE the department store, next to a pair of mannequins Nick found unsettling. Their features were vaguely alien—and sinister, as if they spent the hours after closing plotting the downfall of humankind.

"This is where we part ways," Tess announced cheerfully.

"It is?" Nick was confused. She'd had a very definite opinion about his hair, yet didn't care what clothes he selected? "I thought this was the montage where I try on outfits for your approval while some cheesy pop song is playing."

Tess shook her head. "Nope. Bailey and I are going to check out that merry-go-round at the other end of the mall. If you want a second opinion on clothes, there are friendly sales associates I bet would be eager to help."

"Ah." So he was being ditched because Tess wanted him to practice flirting, which would be tough with an audience of his daughter and a woman mistaken for his significant other.

"Text me when you're done here," Tess said, "but take your time."

"You say that now." He cocked his head toward his daughter. "Someone can be a real handful."

Tess laughed. "You're talking to the original 'unruly handful.' According to my mother, at least. Trust me, I can keep up."

While Nick had always been grateful for the help his mother gave him with Bailey, Erin Calhoun was the first to admit she was no longer the young woman who'd raised three boys. Her granddaughter wore her out quickly. After a few hours in Tess's exuberant company, he was developing a finer appreciation for the reasons Bay wanted a mom. Renewed determination surged through him. He was going to follow whatever instructions Tess gave him and brave the dating world. Whether Farrah fell for him or not, Bailey wouldn't grow up motherless simply because her father was too skittish to speak to women.

He met Tess's gaze. "Got any last-minute advice?"

"Be yourself, just not *yourself.*"

"I should have been more specific. Got any advice that makes sense?"

Intrigued, Bailey stopped turning circles at Tess's side. "You give me advice in ballet class. Are you teaching Daddy about dancing?"

"No, this is different advice." Tess lifted her chin, doing her best to look somber. "I am a woman of much wisdom."

Bailey frowned, her small forehead crinkled in confusion. Nick laughed outright.

"Hey!" Tess jabbed him in the shoulder. "Show some respect for the wise woman."

He grinned down at her. "Aren't wise women usually old and wrinkled? You're…" His gaze slid over her, from her warm brown eyes to her wraparound navy dress, and his words evaporated.

It wasn't a complete shock that she had such a delectably curvy little body—most of the times he saw her she was wearing a leotard and tights, after all. But he was usually in a hurry, ready to spend time with his daughter after a long day and often preoccupied with formulating dinner plans. And Tess was frequently talking to other parents or students, flashing him a smile from across the studio lobby. Though he saw her every single week, he now realized he hadn't truly been looking at her. Suddenly, it—

Oh, hell. He was having one of those, what had she called it earlier? *A lightbulb moment.*

"Nick?" Her voice was soft, more tentative than he'd ever heard it, and her cheeks were scarlet.

Words failed him, as they so often did. He wished he knew how to express how lovely she was without insulting her by sounding stunned. He didn't want to offend her. Nor did he want to sound like his slick, skirt-chasing brother, doling out compliments to any woman who crossed his path.

He cleared his throat. "You… You were going to explain your cryptic statement? About being me but not?"

"Right. While you want to step outside your comfort zone—"

"I do?" he asked wryly.

"Yes. It builds character." Her smile was wide enough to show off her dimples, and he was glad to see her relaxed again, the unwanted tension between them dispelled. "You need clothes that aren't your usual chambray button-downs or shirts with the Galloping C logo. But you don't want to go *so* far outside your norm that you're self-conscious. A man at ease is an attractive man."

"What's attractive?" Bailey interrupted.

"It means women will like him."

"Oh, good!" Bailey clapped her hands together. "If a grown-up lady really, *really* likes him, I might get a new mommy like Suzie."

Nick groaned, eager to change the subject. "Don't you two have a merry-go-round to find?"

"We're leaving," Tess said, her expression apologetic.

Alone, he wandered farther down the tiled path that segmented accessories from appliances. A sharply dressed salesclerk in head-to-toe black appeared from nowhere, like a coyote who'd scented an injured calf.

"Can I interest you in our new signature fragrance?" Without waiting for an answer, she misted him with cologne.

Blehhh. He coughed, enveloped in a cloyingly sweet cloud. What self-respecting man wanted to smell like this?

"Not for me," he managed, lengthening his stride while she tried to convince him to buy the four-piece collection. Shower gel, deodorant *and* aftershave, all matching the cologne? In Nick's opinion, if a man stunk bad enough to need four combined products to fix it, he should just live in seclusion and not inflict himself on folks.

He slowed once he found himself amid racks of clothes with no idea where to start.

"May I help you, sir?"

Turning warily, he checked to ensure that the auburn-haired woman wasn't wielding a spray bottle. "Umm…"

Tess had encouraged him to be himself. *What I am is a retail-averse cowboy with less than no interest in fashion and vague hopes of impressing a woman.* Well, he could work with that.

"Lord, I hope so." He gave her the most winning smile he could muster; she looked dazed for a second, then smiled back. "I'm not real sure what I'm doin' and I'd love to get your opinion. I'd like to find something appropriate for, say, a first date with a special lady."

"Oh." The woman peered up at him from beneath her lashes. "Lucky girl."

By the time Nick rejoined Tess and Bailey, he had two new shirts, a pair of slacks and a grudging appreciation for the mall. Granted, it would never be his favorite place in the world, but the past hour hadn't been nearly the painful experience he'd anticipated. Janette, the auburn-haired salesclerk, had been a huge help. Maybe the friendly smiles she'd showered on him and the way she batted her eyelashes were because she worked on commission, but she'd seemed genuinely drawn to him. Then there'd been the woman who stopped him on his way out to ask if he'd shrug into a jacket she was considering as a gift.

"For my brother," she'd been quick to add. "Not a husband. I'm single." She was trying to get an idea of fit and said he was tall like her brother.

Perspective was everything. As the shortest male in his family, Nick rarely viewed himself as tall. *You are when you're with Tess.* At her height, she would only barely be able to rest her head against his shoulder. Not that she had any reason to do so, Nick reminded himself, blinking the image away.

Tess and Bailey had finished with the merry-go-round and he'd received a text that they'd moved on to the children's arcade across from the movie theater. They were playing air hockey as he approached, and Bailey spotted him first.

"Daddy!" She rushed toward him, colliding into him with one of her patented tackle-hugs, chatting a mile a minute about all of the things they'd done and seen. "I love the mall."

"It's not half-bad," he conceded.

"Does that mean you're glad we came?" Tess asked.

"It's certainly been a productive day," he said. And the ego boost hadn't sucked. "We accomplished everything on our list. Plus, this place sells cinnamon rolls the size of small planets. Who wouldn't enjoy that? But we should probably head home now," he told his daughter.

Her face fell. "I don't wanna leave. Besides, you said you'd take me to the movie."

"What movie?" Nick didn't recall making any such promise.

She pointed toward the opposite wall, at a poster for an animated movie about a cowboy cat and his adventures with his talking horse. "We saw a commercial on TV and I asked if we could see it and you said you'd take me."

"And I will, eventually. That doesn't mean today. Miss Tess probably has dance classes to teach this evening."

"Actually," Tess interjected, "I follow the school district's calendar. On teacher in-service days like today, I close the studio since some families use the opportunity for a mini-holiday."

"And you really want to spend your day off watching a cartoon cat?" Nick asked.

Her smile was sheepish. "I was planning to see it anyway. At least with a kid in tow, I don't feel so silly about it."

Backed by an ally, Bailey pushed her advantage. "So can we, Daddy? Please, please, *please!*"

Why not? After all, he himself was in no real hurry to end their day. He met Tess's gaze. "Are you sure about this?"

"I never say anything I don't mean, remember?"

"Yes!" Bailey pumped her small fist into the air.

Worried his excited daughter might run headlong through pedestrian traffic in her enthusiasm, Nick scooped her up with his free arm. "We still have to check showtimes," he said.

"Okay." Bailey snugged against him then pulled back in surprise. "Daddy, why do you smell like apples?"

"I was spotted by the enemy," he said. "A woman all in black ambushed me—an honest-to-goodness perfume-counter ninja."

"That's nothing," Tess deadpanned, her sparkling eyes at odds with her solemn expression. "You should see the ruthless samurai warriors who work in Swimwear."

Chapter Six

Laughter erupted through the theater, making Tess realize that the on-screen feline in spurs and a cowboy hat must have drawled something funny. She'd missed it, too distracted by Nick's proximity. Somewhere between now and the "coming soon" previews, part of her brain had forgotten this wasn't a date. It had been too long since Tess had sat in the cool, dark intimacy of a movie theater with a good-looking man's arm around her.

It's not around you. It's just casually draped over the back of your seat. Which was apparently close enough for her pinging hormones.

Tess tried telling herself that the fluttery sensation in the pit of her stomach was simple biology, caused by the total lack of space between seats. Nick's thigh grazed hers every time he moved. And since he was trying to see over his kindergarten daughter, who was incapable of being still, he moved a lot. Bailey had abandoned her own chair ten minutes into the movie, seeking comfort from her father when the movie's menacing villain had burned down a town.

Nick had obligingly cuddled his daughter against his chest. "Don't worry, kiddo, justice will prevail."

One might think the presence of a six-year-old chaperone would help keep the mood platonic. Tess, however, had always adored children and considered being good with kids a very desirable trait in a man. Watching Nick with his little girl made her feel all gooey inside.

At least he was wearing pretentious cologne. It wasn't nearly as heady as the masculine combination of sunshine and leather, the way he'd smelled when he'd helped her dismount from her horse the other day. His hands had grazed over her denim-clad hips, and she'd nearly shivered. Sternly reminding herself it was no more than he did for dozens of tourists every year, she'd squelched her inappropriate reaction.

At the moment, it was proving unsquelchable.

Nick leaned in close, his voice a whisper. "Not having a good time?" His breath feathered over her sensitive ear, intangible contact that nonetheless rippled through her body.

She inhaled sharply. "I'm having... This is, um, great. Really."

"You seem subdued. Highly unlike you." His gaze went back to the screen, and he grinned with boyish enthusiasm. "Shoot-out scene! My kind of movie."

Tess forced herself to focus on the climactic showdown instead of the fleeting and completely foolish dizziness she'd felt when Nick had been so near. Near enough to kiss. She blinked, distracted all over again. The next thing she knew, credits were rolling and Bailey was tugging on her hand.

"This was the best day ever," the little girl announced. "And guess what?"

"What?" Tess asked, hoping for more whimsical conversation about ninjas, something silly to lighten her mood.

Bailey beamed at her. "I've decided *you* should be my new mommy."

NICK WASN'T SURPRISED by Tess's hasty goodbye when they pulled up in her driveway. She was clearly embarrassed by his daughter's earlier suggestion. Rather than respond to

Bailey's outlandish idea at the theater, Tess had excused herself by saying she needed the ladies' room. Then she'd sprinted away from them with the speed of a Thoroughbred racehorse. Nick had opted to table the discussion until later.

In the truck, Tess had asked Bailey lots of questions about kindergarten and the ranch, keeping the girl engaged while clearly directing conversation away from marriage. Nick suspected Tess hadn't wanted to say anything that would hurt Bay's feelings. But now that he and his daughter were alone, it was his parental duty to make sure she understood reality.

He glanced in the rearview mirror at his daughter. Her face was wreathed in utter contentment after her day of fun.

"I had a good time today," he began. "I always have fun when I'm with you. You're the most important person in my life, Bailey. I want you to be happy. I know you'd like me to get married, but that might not happen."

Trying to head off the scowl he saw forming, he added quickly, "It *might* happen. But not for a long time. Sometimes men and women date for years before they decide to get married. It's a very serious decision, and before I could ever take a step like that, I'd have to make sure the woman in question loved you as much as I do."

"Miss Tess loves me," Bailey said confidently.

"True, but Miss Tess isn't my girlfriend. You know that, right? I'm not dating her."

Bay shot him that look all kids got when exasperated by the idiocy of adults. "Why not?"

Because... As he thought about the beautiful redhead who'd been making him smile all day, he was suddenly hardpressed for an answer.

ON SATURDAY MORNINGS, Tess worked the studio's reception desk while a nineteen-year-old taught a hip-hop class to preteens. For half an hour, the phone rang steadily, but then it got quiet. Tess had just accepted a late tuition payment from an apologetic Parker Casteel when she realized she was all caught up on emails and messages. She decided to hit the vending machine for some caffeine. Tess hadn't been sleeping as well as usual and was fighting the unprofessional urge to take a nap at her desk.

When she returned with a cold can of soda, she noticed that Farrah Landon had joined the other two moms waiting in the lobby, both of whom were silently reading books. The conversation Farrah was having on her cell phone carried.

"I desperately need a night out," Farrah was saying. "Saturday nights should be fun! Do you think your husband would let me borrow you for the evening if I can find a sitter?"

Obviously, Tess wasn't the only one engaged in benign eavesdropping. As soon as Farrah disconnected her call, one of the other moms cleared her throat. "I couldn't help overhearing…are you looking for a sitter? We've been using Eden Winchester—the Ranger's daughter? She's saving up for a car and usually jumps at the chance to earn some money. I don't know if she'll be available on such short notice, but I can give you her number."

"That would be super! I love my girls, but the youngest needs so much one-on-one attention and the oldest is hitting that moody stage. They're exhausting. And my ex is completely useless," she added bitterly.

As time moved closer to class dismissal, more parents and guardians filed into the studio. Despite the increased buzz of noise and activity, Tess heard most of Farrah's follow-up call to her friend, confirming a girls' night at a locally owned beer-and-burger joint that featured pool tables and darts. It was like the universe was giving Tess a sign. She'd planned to nudge Nick and Farrah together at the Valentine's performance—maybe pairing them up to help with the lights or set out refreshments together—and this was a golden opportunity for her to lay some groundwork.

Impatience simmered inside her, but she knew she couldn't call Nick from the studio. She needed to wait until lunch, when she could dial his cell phone from the privacy of her car. He didn't know it yet, but he was taking her out tonight.

THE SIGHT OF TESS'S NAME and number had Nick smiling as he stripped off his work gloves to answer the touch-screen phone. "Hello?" He leaned against the section of fence he'd just finished repairing, glad neither of his brothers were here to catch him grinning like an idiot.

"It's time to implement Phase Two!"

"Of what, your plan for world domination?"

"Don't be ridiculous. My plan to take over the world is already *well* past the second stage. I'm talking about your courtship of one Ms. Farrah Landon."

Right. He should have guessed that immediately. After all, the only phone conversations he and Tess had ever shared stemmed from his interest in Farrah. "Dare I ask what Phase Two entails?"

"You remember when you told me asking a woman to go out with you isn't as difficult as sustaining conversation through the whole date? You proved yourself capable of casual chatting at the mall. That was like an animated short. Now it's time for the full-length film—dinner with a woman. Specifically, me."

Before he had a chance to process her unexpected declaration, she added, "I happen to know where Farrah will be tonight."

"Oh, Lord. Are you stalking her? I'm having unsettling mental images of you shadowing her to her car and digging through her trash for clues."

"Okay, first, *ew*. And second, maybe you should watch more nature documentaries and fewer police procedurals. I'm not stalking anyone!" Indignation sharpened her tone. "She was broadcasting a private conversation in public. I've never seen her when she didn't have that phone in hand. Honestly, she's probably one of those women who even takes calls in the— Sorry. Not the point."

"I get why a practice dinner might be a good idea. But why does it matter where Farrah is?"

"Because one way for a woman to notice a man is attractive is to see him attracting someone else."

"We're trying to make her jealous?"

"Not exactly. It's more like... Say you walk by a horse in a stable. It doesn't really catch your attention. It's a perfectly fine horse, but nothing about it jumps out at you on first glance. But later, you see someone riding the same horse and realize how much spirit and grace it has. Suddenly, you're intrigued. I know it's short notice, but can you find a sitter for Bailey tonight?"

"Almost definitely." He didn't think his mom had plans but, given her frequent hints about his dating life or lack thereof, he suspected she'd rearrange her entire social calendar if necessary.

"Wonderful. Pick me up at seven. Wear one of your new shirts."

He grinned, already looking forward to the evening. "You're very bossy, Contessa."

"Try to think of it as an endearing quirk."

"Yes, ma'am."

"Wow." Heather Winchester stood on Tess's front porch, beaming. "You look incredible."

"Crap."

"Um...did I say something wrong?"

"I feel like I'm trying too hard." Tess reached out to take the box of altered ballet costumes from her friend. Heather's full-time job was at an art gallery, but she did steady side business as a seamstress. "I don't want to look *too* nice."

"Oh." Heather followed her inside. "Then you missed the mark, because you've never been more beautiful."

"Some help you are," Tess groused. "If you really loved me, you'd tell me I look mediocre at best."

"No can do. Given our past, I promised Zane—and myself—that I'd never lie again. Not even little white lies."

Tess had never been completely clear on the details but she knew that when Heather had first met her Texas Ranger husband, she'd had to deceive him about who she was to protect her daughter Josie from some unsavory people. "You want a glass of wine while I go change?" *Again.*

"Tempting. I can't stay long, though. How about half a glass?"

"Perfect. I'll drink the other half."

Tess's kitchen was tiny, but the sunlight spilling through the large picture window created an airy illusion of space. She pulled down two blue-stemmed wineglasses and retrieved a mellow pinot grigio from the fridge, leaving her friend to pour while she darted back to her room and swapped the deceptively simple black dress for a dark denim skirt and turquoise peasant blouse.

She hurried back into the kitchen, the tile floor cool against the soles of her feet. "Better?" she demanded. "By which I mean, worse?"

Heather leaned back in her chair, considering. "The blouse is a great color for you and the skirt shows off legs honed by years of ballet. I think you're just gonna have to accept that you're gorgeous. You could try another outfit, but it's not really the clothes. There's something…" She stared hard at Tess's face. "Who's the mystery guy who put that sparkle in your eyes, the one you're hoping to impress without being too obvious?"

"No guy!" Tess took the seat opposite her friend. "Well, technically, there is a guy, but not like you're suggesting. I'm having dinner with Nick Calhoun to discuss a…project we're working on."

"Farrah Landon?"

Tess nearly spilled her wine. "How'd you know?" Nick was a private person. If he thought other people were gossiping about their arrangement…

"Lorelei mentioned it. But only because you and I are so close! The way she brought it up, I think she assumed you'd already told me. After all, I know firsthand what a matchmaker you are."

"I didn't do a thing to introduce you to Zane," Tess said, temporarily diverted. "I didn't have to—you were living right next door to him!"

"True, but you pushed me to give him a chance every darn time you talked to me."

"And now you're happily married." Tess raised her glass in a salute to the happy couple. "I am great at figuring out who people belong with."

"If you say so."

Tess bristled. "When have I ever been wrong?"

"Maybe you're not, but… Never mind. You've lived here your entire life, and it's only been a year for me. I don't know Farrah very well. I wouldn't have an impression of her at all except that her youngest was in class with Josie at the beginning of the year. Then they hired that new teacher and shuffled some—"

"What is your impression? Of Farrah?"

Heather bit her lip. "She's very flashy. Take that two-door sports car she drives. It's sleek and sexy but when I see her in the carpool line, it just seems impractical. You should have seen her older daughter trying to climb out of the backseat with her science-fair project. Not that you have to drive a minivan to be a good mom! I don't think she's evil or anything."

"It's okay," Tess said. "I asked for your opinion, remember?"

A moment later, Heather continued. "Her clothes are all name brand. And, correct me if I'm wrong, but I think she lives in the most expensive subdivision in town. Isn't Nick more subdued? I guess I just have trouble imagining her being drawn to him. Seems like she'd be instinctively attracted to the 'hot' brother."

"Nick *is* the hot Calhoun brother!"

At Tess's fervent tone, Heather's eyebrows shot up.

Tess could feel her cheeks blazing. "You know how protective I get of my friends," she mumbled.

"Uh-huh." Heather rose, her expression amused. "I should be going. One last piece of unsolicited advice on your appearance tonight?"

"Sure."

"Wear some of that kiss-proof lipstick that won't smear. Just in case."

Chapter Seven

Even though Tess had suggested Nick wear some of his new clothes, she must have subconsciously been expecting a pair of his regular jeans and a Western shirt with a small Galloping C logo above the pocket. Because the sight of him in black slacks, a tightly woven hunter-green shirt and lightweight leather jacket was staggering. Clean shaven and with his hair recently cut, he was like an alternate version of himself. Everything she'd found desirable about him was still there but now combined with a new air of sophistication, mystery.

Tess swallowed, her greeting forgotten.

At her silence, Nick's smile faded. "Am I late? Early?"

"You're perfect. Um, right on time."

His voice lowered, taking on a husky familiarity. "You look fantastic."

Their eyes met, and Tess struggled to find a response. Speechlessness was not typically a problem for her. By the time common sense kicked in and she realized the logical reply was "thank you," too many moments had passed, rendering the answer awkward. Crud. Would he think her rude now, unappreciative of the compliment? She was supposed to be encouraging him! Busy second-guessing herself, she didn't quite register his question until he repeated it.

"Ready to go?" he asked for the second time.

Lord. Two minutes into the evening and she was already wishing for a do-over. Was this how Nick often felt, uncertain of what to say and how others might react to him? It was an awful sensation, something that squirmed in her abdomen as if she'd swallowed a bucket of live tadpoles.

"I am definitely ready to get out of here," she said. Having him stand on her front porch was too intimate somehow, as if she might invite him in at any moment. Once they were at the pool hall, she'd regain her equilibrium.

She used her key to lock the dead bolt, trying not to notice how close he was standing. But it was impossible to ignore the warmth from his body, the smell of his skin, something indefinable and entirely Nick beneath the manufactured fragrances of soap and shampoo. Tess inhaled deeply. Then, deciding it was tacky to be sniffing her date, she spun on the heel of her sandal and marched toward his truck.

He followed, reaching to open the door for her at the exact moment she gripped the handle. His hand was strong and callused over hers. A tingling warmth coursed through her, and her mouth went dry.

"Doesn't a gentleman get the door for his date?" he asked softly.

"Absolutely." She flashed him a bright smile, making an effort to relax. "So far, A-plus on your test run. Phase Two, all systems go."

He grinned. "I feel like we need a code name."

By the time he rounded the truck to get in on the driver's side, she'd regained her composure. "Operation Cupid?" she suggested. "Count yourself lucky the only arrows we'll be using are metaphorical. My limited experience with archery was pure disaster. I'm pretty sure there's a picture of me in the administrative offices of Camp Falcon Rock, Most Failed Camper Ever to Pass Through."

"Would this be the same camp of your much-lamented riding experiences?"

"Falcon Rock's the official name. To me, it'll always be a little piece of Hell on Earth. I didn't want to go in the first place, but my parents insisted. They were trying to get my mind off—" She stopped abruptly.

Tess was by no means an introvert, nor was she shy about expressing her opinion—whether asked for or not. But she never discussed this with anyone. She'd never figured out a way to talk about it that didn't make her sound self-pitying or resentful of her sister.

Braking for the stop sign at the top of her street, Nick slid her a questioning glance. "My parents used to force me into activities in an effort to 'get me out of my shell.' I doubt *your* folks had to worry about that."

"No, my being sentenced to camp was an attempt to distract me from ballet. My sister and I had both auditioned for a prestigious summer company. Regina got into her age class. I didn't." She tried to sound nonchalant about ancient history, completely unbothered that her sister had gone on to a successful career in Tess's chosen field. "I'd been psyching myself up for months. Being accepted into that company would have been like Christmas and my birthday and Mardi Gras all rolled into one. Regina only decided to try out at the last minute, after she and her boyfriend broke up, freeing up a lot of her time."

Nick made a sympathetic noise. After a moment, he offered, "Siblings can be real jackasses, can't they?"

His observation startled a laugh from her. "I refuse to answer that on the grounds it may incriminate me."

"Don't get me wrong," he said. "I love my brothers. But it was difficult being the 'runt of the litter.' The youngest, the one with the speech impairment, the one who came last in school. With every teacher I ever had, I felt as if I were either trying to live up to Wyatt's reputation or live down Kevin's. He was more of a troublemaker, although he was always able to talk himself out of the worst scrapes. I don't think he's been at a loss for words a day in his life. Can I admit something awful?"

"Oh, please do."

"I think proposing to Marla was even more exciting because I knew neither of my brothers had ever popped the question. Obviously, that's not the driving reason I wanted to marry her, but it was an added rush. I was doing something first, succeeding in an area they hadn't. Of course, then she left me," he added ruefully, "which restored the natural order of the universe. Or, at least, the Calhoun family."

"What exactly happened between the two of you?" Tess probably shouldn't pry, but when had she ever let that stop her?

He considered his words carefully. "Marla grew up poor in an Oklahoma trailer park. She got to college on scholarships and worked multiple part-time jobs so that she could live with some style. Much as she was infatuated with the idea of my family's ranch and that we owned so much land, she tired of the reality pretty quickly. She was cut out more for country clubs than country living. Her leaving made me wonder…"

If he should have done something differently? "You can't blame yourself for her choices," Tess said. Granted, she didn't know what kind of husband Nick had been, but she felt as if she knew enough about him as a person and a father to make an educated guess.

"That's not what I meant, but thanks."

He was about to make the last turn before they reached their destination, and Tess sensed he'd be less forthcoming with personal details once they were surrounded by a crowd. This was her best opportunity for learning more about Nick and his ex-wife. Not that she cared much about the woman she'd only seen a couple of times in passing, but she definitely cared about Nick Calhoun. Far more than she'd realized.

"What did you mean?" she blurted. "What did you wonder after the divorce?"

"I wonder if I ever should have married her in the first place." He sighed. "If she was truly The One, I probably should have missed her more once she was gone. I would have been faithful, would have honored my vows. But did I really love her enough to justify a lifelong commitment? We met first day on campus, when neither of us knew anyone yet. We were neighbors and ended up with classes together. There was a certain degree of convenience to our relationship. No, that sounds cold. I did care about her, very much."

"You were comfortable with her," Tess translated.

He nodded. "I felt at ease around her. For me, that was a big deal. But if I was so in love with her, shouldn't it have been harder to get over her? I rarely even think about her, except to wish she made more effort to contact Bay. I was angry she abandoned us, but never really grief-stricken. Does that make me shallow?"

"It makes you someone who married young and is functioning as best you can as a single dad. I don't see any crime in that."

"Thanks." He eased the truck into a parking spot, then shot her a look of pure gratitude. "You're a really good friend, you know that?"

"Yeah." A wave of irrational gloom washed over her. "I know."

NICK SEEMED ENDEARINGLY nervous once they'd been shown to a booth by the hostess, almost as if this were a real date. Or, perhaps, Tess realized as the waiter wrote down their drink choices, his nerves were caused by Farrah Landon. She sat with a friend at a table on the far side of the dining room.

After the waiter had left to get their beverages, Nick scanned the menu. "Should I try to order for both of us?"

"Do you have any idea what I want?"

"Not really."

She arched a brow, her lips twitching. "And do I seem incapable of making decisions for myself?"

He chuckled. "Not at all."

"Then it would be pretty dumb for you to order for me," she chided lightly. "I'm not sure how that myth got started, that it's macho for a man to pick out what the little lady will have. It's more effective—and sometimes downright sexy— to ask a woman what she likes."

His gaze locked with hers. "Are we still talking about dinner?"

"Um…" Tess was grateful that the waiter returned with her glass of wine, interrupting conversation.

After they'd both ordered, Nick asked, "So, what *do* you like? In a guy, I mean. What do you want in a relationship?"

His question caught her off guard.

"C'mon," he coaxed. "We've spent a lot of time talking about my love life. It's only fair that I ask about yours, right?"

She couldn't fault his logic. Stalling, she sipped her wine. "It's not like groceries. I haven't made a list."

"So make one now," he invited. "You have to have some idea. If ever there was a woman who knew her own mind…"

What was she looking for in a man? Draining her glass, she pondered some of the couples she knew. She skipped over her parents' own unbalanced marriage, where her mother announced decisions as if they were royal decrees and her father mostly kept his head down and tried to stay clear of any female drama. Tess wanted a true partnership, like some of her friends had found.

Sam Travis looked at Lorelei as if she were the most gorgeous woman alive, which was close to true; she had to at least be in the top twenty. Newlyweds Zane and Heather Winchester, who'd each learned from failed first marriages, shared a deep bond, an understanding that would lead outsiders to assume they'd been together for decades. Then there was Tess's sister. In addition to synchronized life goals, Regina and her choreographer husband were an exquisitely matched set. Seeing them together made Tess think of priceless bookends, but they were so unerringly dignified that she secretly found them a bit creepy. Did they ever laugh together?

"Someone I can have fun with," she said decisively. "But a good listener, too, someone who can be playful but intuit when it's time to take what I'm saying seriously. A man who makes my toes curl whenever we…kiss. Someone who believes I'm worth the trouble of pursuing." She recalled men she'd seen court her sister. Tess wasn't the type to play hard to get—she either liked a guy or she didn't—but it would be nice to know he thought her worth proving himself.

"Oh, and he has to be good with kids, obviously." She bit the inside of her lip, wishing she could take back the words. Did they sound like a come-on, given that Nick was absolutely wonderful with his daughter? "I—I've always wanted children. When Regina got married, I hoped I'd soon have nieces and nephews to spoil, but she's adamant about waiting. She doesn't want motherhood to interfere with her dancing career."

Nick swirled his drink around, not meeting her eyes. "Speaking of kids…I should apologize about what Bailey said the other day. About you being her new mother?"

Mortification stung her cheeks. "No apology necessary." She didn't want to sit through a mutual affirmation of there being nothing romantic between her and Nick. Knowing he didn't see her "that way" was fine; trying to smile across the table as he voiced it aloud would be humiliating.

The waiter appeared with their salads. "Anyone want grated cheese? Freshly ground pepper? Another glass of wine, ma'am?"

"Yes, please."

Blessedly, once the waiter had bustled off, Nick didn't resume the topic of Bailey and her impulsive announcement. Instead, he returned to the subject of Tess's list.

"You have a good handle on relationships," he said admiringly. "Some people have unreasonable expectations—they look for perfection and are doomed to be unhappy. Other people are just grateful for any tenderness and settle for less than they deserve. You won't do that."

"I won't?" She certainly had no intentions of doing so, but she was nonplussed by the ringing conviction in his voice.

"Hell, no. You're direct and brave enough to follow your heart." He frowned, glancing toward the table where Farrah sat.

Was he wishing he'd had the gumption to ask her out before now? Was he realizing that, if he had, he could even now be seated across from the woman he'd dreamed of going out with for more than a decade, instead of getting advice from a busybody who hadn't even been in a relationship since…

Her mind blanked as she tried to calculate how long it had been. Lord, was that depressing.

Midway through her second glass of wine, Tess began to feel slightly less depressed. How bad could her social life be if she was sitting here with one of the hottest guys in town, a man who kept nodding at her as if her every word was a pearl? A pleasant buzz stole through her, subtly blurring her thoughts until they were like an alluring watercolor.

She was enjoying her delicious steak and once again

feeling her buoyant self when Nick asked suddenly, "What makes a great kiss, one that would curl your toes?"

"I— What now?"

"Your hypothetical criteria was that he be an incredible… kisser." Nick's slight pause and smirk made it clear he knew her thoughts had gone further than that, even if she'd only given him the PG version.

Knowing how easily she blushed, Tess tried very hard not to dwell on what qualities made a man an incredible lover— and tried equally hard not to wonder just how many of those qualities Nick Calhoun possessed. "Um, some things aren't easily captured in words," she demurred.

Mischief glimmered in his eyes. "Are you saying it would be easier to demonstrate than to explain?"

She froze, the idea of him kissing her all too vivid.

"Don't worry, I was teasing," he assured her. "That would go above and beyond the call of duty."

"Not like it would be a hardship," she muttered.

He learned forward in his chair, the earlier humor in his gaze replaced by a more predatory gleam. "Are you saying you'd want me to kiss you?"

"It's crossed my mind." The errant words were out before she could censor herself—not that she'd ever employed much of a verbal filter. "Ignore me. I'm on my second glass of wine."

He shook a finger at her. "You never say anything you don't mean. Isn't that your mantra?"

She could flirt with him, tell herself it was in the name of "coaching" him. Farrah could look over at any moment and see the two of them smiling together, Nick showing a seductive side of himself. But the idea of playacting the truth scraped Tess raw. She felt exposed and queasy.

"I think the smart thing for me to do is shut up," she said firmly. "Radio silence."

"An impulse I can understand, but aren't we supposed to be practicing the art of conversation?"

"Think of this as a disaster drill," she instructed. "What if you're on a date and the discussion goes south? Do you have a contingency plan?"

He considered her challenge, then startled her by scooting his chair back. Standing, he extended one hand toward her.

"What are you doing?"

"This is my plan B." He tilted his head toward the live band and small dance floor through the archway. "I figure we can let the music do the talking for us. Dance with me."

"But…" She'd been aiming for strategic retreat, a little distance between them. Sliding into his embrace was *not* what she had in mind. "We haven't finished dinner yet."

He signaled to the waiter, summarizing the situation in quick pantomime. "Our plates will be safe for five minutes. C'mon, you're the best dancer in town. Are you really going to leave me hanging here? People are watching." He gave her a lopsided smile that was somehow both cocky and lovable. It was the smile Kevin had been attempting his entire life yet never quite capturing. "What will it do to my reputation if everyone sees you reject me? All your hard work reinventing me, undone."

"Oh, fine!" Her acceptance came out in a soft snarl that belied the flutter of anticipation she felt. Dancing was as natural to her as breathing, and the idea of swirling around the floor, her limbs tangled with Nick's, was damned exhilarating.

And the song the band had just started was fast, not one of those sappy love ballads that caused "dancers" to just sway in place. Some claimed slow dances were the most romantic, but Tess found them to be awkward and pointless. Dancing was meant for bodies to *move,* to feel, to push limits.

On the floor, Nick took her hand in his, splaying his other

hand against her back. "Keep up now, Contessa." Then he gave her the most devastating grin she'd ever seen. It lique-fied her; only years of discipline kept her steady on her feet.

He spun her into a brisk modified polka. Her heart raced, and heat coursed through her. *Left, right, left. Right, left, right.* All while whirring in tightly controlled circles that kept her curves pressed to his broad body, hard with muscles carved from hours of manual labor. One of his legs was be-tween hers, as much as the denim of her skirt would allow, and she felt the briefest twinge of embarrassment that he might guess how the contact affected her. But there was no chance for embarrassment to take root. Not when Tess was having the time of her life.

She was flying, tethered to the world only by the hold of the most attractive man she knew. When she'd seen him on horseback, she'd thought him in his element. But that was before she'd seen him on a dance floor. His body worked in perfect choreography with hers, their inherent rhythm su-perseding the notes produced by the band. They moved in a pulse and tempo no longer dictated by the music, and she never wanted to stop. Her lungs burned as they spun faster, the need to catch her breath secondary to the harmony of two sublimely attuned bodies completing one motion.

When the song stopped, Nick led her in one last spin for good measure, then dipped her dramatically. Years of accu-mulated skill allowed her to bend nearly to the floor with-out overbalancing them. Spontaneous applause surrounded them, and Tess straightened. She'd never been intimidated by performing in front of an audience but suddenly she felt an unfamiliar stab of shyness. Probably because what she and Nick had just publicly shared felt far more intimate than simple dancing, as if they'd done something illicit in front of their neighbors.

Easily a dozen people were staring at them—including

Farrah Landon, whose eyes were wide. It was commonplace to see Wyatt or Kevin Calhoun cut a rug with a date but watching Nick masterfully navigate the dance floor was a rare sight. Tess had never needed to offer him advice about women or drag him to the mall in the next county. All it had taken was three minutes and an up-tempo song.

"Plan B, huh?" She forced herself to move away from him, breathing hard. "More like your secret weapon."

Chapter Eight

Nick tried to focus on what Tess had just said to him, but he couldn't think. *Liar.* He was thinking plenty—about the feel of Tess's lush body, the temptation of what her mouth might taste like, the desire to sink into her. He was shell-shocked, watching her mouth move but not really hearing her words over the dull roar in his ears. What were the odds she'd just said, "Take me, Nick"?

He cleared his throat. "Wh-what?"

"I said, why didn't you tell me you could dance like that?"

"I don't. Usually." Not like that.

He knew how to dance. With all the town festivals and outdoor concerts, it was difficult to grow up here without learning the fundamentals, plus Erin had given all three of her boys some pointers. But he'd wondered if he would be out of practice.

Instead, everything he'd ever known had come rushing back to him the moment Tess stepped into his arms…along with a few things he wasn't sure he'd known in the first place. She was living inspiration, motivation for a man to do his level best.

They returned to their table. Neither of them showed any interest in their food, but they both gulped down glasses of water. Nick flagged down the waiter to request more.

The waiter smiled at Tess. "Bravo! I feel like I should ask you for your autographs after that performance."

Tess ducked her head. "Just letting off some steam."

Nick bit his tongue, battling back suggestions of other ways they could release some steam if she was interested. *Was* she interested? Tess was so naturally outgoing and friendly that a man with limited dating experience might misread her. Had he imagined the sudden huskiness of her voice earlier when she'd said kissing him wouldn't be a hardship? He'd put himself on the line by asking if that meant she wanted to kiss him.

It's crossed my mind.

That wasn't specifically a yes, but it sure wasn't a denial. He cast an involuntary glance at Farrah Landon, recalling just why Tess had invited him out tonight. Catching his eye, Farrah gave him a coy little finger wave that left him bemused.

It was difficult to recall why he'd felt so drawn to Farrah. Nostalgia, combined with their bond as two single parents who had survived divorce and were each raising daughters? He'd asked Tess tonight for specific qualities she would require in a relationship. Why had he never thought to ask himself that question? Hell, Bailey probably had a clearer idea of who he should date than he did.

Which brought him back to Tess.

He turned his gaze back to her, finding her expression shadowed. "Everything okay?"

"Long day," she said weakly. "I was at the studio all day, now this."

He felt his disappointment clear to the pit of his stomach. "So no chance of my talking you into another dance?"

"Actually, I think I'd rather leave now, unless you want to stay for dessert." She rallied, flashing him a smile. "But don't worry. I think we already accomplished our goal in coming here tonight."

Nick didn't answer. He wasn't sure how to explain that they were no longer working toward the same goal.

I AM HAPPY FOR my friend. I am truly and genuinely happy for my friend. Staring out the passenger window even though it was too dark to see the Texas landscape, Tess grappled with déjà vu. Why did it seem as if lately she'd had to give herself these pep talks often, as if she had to compel herself to be glad for others' good fortune? Was she becoming bitter and jealous? Just because everyone was pairing up as decisively as the animals boarding Noah's Ark and she was standing out in the flood with a pair of flippers and a snorkel...

Get a grip, Fitzpatrick. No one likes a whiner.

She turned toward Nick, forcing cheer into her voice the same way she'd doggedly forced her hips into those old jeans to go riding. "In case I forgot to say so earlier, I had fun tonight. Did you see the way Farrah was looking at you when we left the dance floor? She wasn't the only one, either."

"That's...great."

Wow, even *she* had sounded more convincing than that. "What's wrong? You know I'm serious about Farrah seeming interested, right?"

"I know. You mean what you say."

"And that's what you wanted, isn't it? To break the ice, build up to finally asking her out after all these years?" She held her breath, wondering how she'd react if he said no, that he'd been wrong.

I was a fool, Tess, for thinking I wanted a lissome blonde with parenting experience and a hot car. I'd much rather be with a round redhead who has madly untamed curls and a tendency to act without thinking. Yeah. She could just imagine what her long-suffering patrician mother would have to say about *that* flight of fancy.

"Don't think I'm ungrateful for all the help you've given me," he said a few seconds later. "I'm glad she noticed me. It just occurs to me that liking the way I dance isn't a basis for anything real. I should be more analytical about this, like you."

"Me?"

"You were very insightful when you talked about the qualities you consider important."

Her innate sense of honesty forced her to point out, "Those were traits I came up with spur of the moment. Subconsciously, you probably have a list like that, too. Even if you've never itemized it, you have an idea of what's important to you and who you like."

He was quiet as they pulled into her neighborhood. Was he having second thoughts about his feelings for Farrah? Or was he just psyching himself out? After all, he'd had a lot of time to build her up in his mind as his Dream Girl. He'd said himself the first time he spoke with Tess on the phone that Farrah might be aiming too high.

Tess was surprised when he parked the truck in her driveway, cut the ignition and removed the key. Her heart leaped in her chest as if it were trying to execute a *grand jeté*. "You're getting out, too?"

He hitched a brow, disgruntled by her surprise. "What self-respecting man doesn't walk his date to the door at the end of the night?"

It wasn't a real date. But she couldn't quite voice the objection because it was difficult to remember which part hadn't been real. The breathless rush she'd experienced in his arms had certainly been genuine. Her nerves before he came to pick her up, as she'd changed clothes six times and fortified herself with wine, had been one hundred percent sincere. And the way she'd felt tonight whenever she glanced across the table and fell into his gaze…

There went her heart again, leaping around like a crazed soloist in search of a spotlight.

Nick opened her door, offering her a hand to climb down from the height of the truck. His fingers rasped against hers, and she inhaled a shaky breath. She quickly drew her hand away on the pretext of fishing her keys from her purse. They walked up the steps together, and she unlocked the door. Should she invite him in for a cup of decaf coffee? Point out that it was a nice evening and ask him to sit on the porch with her, enjoying the song of crickets and the sparkling canvas of stars overhead?

"Tess?" Despite his velvety tone of voice, she jumped as if she'd heard gunfire.

She tried to camouflage her reflex by turning the knob and opening the door with more force than required. "Yes?"

"I think you're right. Maybe deep down, I do know what I want."

"And?" She swallowed.

As if they were on the dance floor again, he pulled her against him, moving to a song only he could hear. Spearing one hand through her wayward curls, he cupped the back of her head and tilted her face toward his. He captured her mouth in a coaxing kiss that bloomed from gentle to searing in the space of a heartbeat. Heat flooded her body. They explored each other with a frenzied thoroughness. Thought became sensation and movement. His thumb skimmed the edge of her breast through the filmy material of her blouse, jolting a sharp current of need through her.

He moved his mouth from hers long enough to trace feathery kisses up the curve of her neck. "We shouldn't be standing in your doorway like this."

Right, because she'd hate for the neighbors to see the hottest guy in town crazed with desire over her. She tugged him into the dimly lit interior of her house and had just slammed the door when she found herself pressed between Nick and the wall. One of his firmly muscled legs was between hers, pushing the edge of her skirt upward. Cool air teased her thighs, and she trembled.

Nick noticed, backing off immediately. He still had one hand curved at the nape of her neck, but he'd put several inches between them when before there'd only been a few thin layers of fabric. "I'm rushing you, aren't I?"

No! Except…now that he'd paused long enough for her to get oxygen to her lust-addled brain, she admitted to herself they were rushing. Was she subconsciously hurrying because she knew that, if she stopped to think, she'd come to her senses?

She exhaled heavily, managing an apologetic half smile. "We shouldn't be doing this."

"Damn." He shoved a hand through his hair, no longer resembling the polished, urbane version of himself who'd shown up here at the beginning of the evening. "I was so hoping you wouldn't say that."

"Me, too," she admitted. "But it's true."

"Tess, I—"

She held up a hand, halting his words. "You can call me tomorrow. Or later in the week. We can talk then." If she didn't do the sensible and honorable thing by kicking him out now, she might yet lose her head. And no amount of physical bliss tonight would be worth the world of regret and misgivings tomorrow.

STARTING OUT THE EVENING, Nick hadn't had any idea what to expect. And now that the night had concluded…well, he wasn't sure what in the hell had just happened. Shifting uncomfortably in the driver's seat, he tried to ignore the lingering demands of his body and focus on driving safely back to the Galloping C.

Had he screwed up by kissing Tess? As he'd told his daughter, he and Tess weren't romantically involved. And only a couple of hours ago, Tess had referred to their date as a "test run." Instead of adhering to reality, he'd gone with sheer instinct and grabbed her.

He couldn't remember the last time he'd blindly followed his instincts with a woman. Ironically, the person he most wanted to turn to for advice now was probably the last one he should ask. Even though only a week had passed since Tess first approached him, he'd quickly fallen into the habit of considering her his romance coach. No, it was more than that. She was a friend.

No. It was more than *that,* too.

When he pulled up to the ranch's main house, lights spilled from various windows. He could see his brothers and father in the living room. Upstairs, softer light shone from behind the pale green curtains of his parents' room. Then there was a telltale gleam in the tiny window of the bathroom. If he was seeking guidance, there was no shortage of people inside he could ask. But Nick had always been the most private of the Calhoun brothers. Kevin had been bragging about his exploits since middle school, and while Wyatt wasn't as obnoxious as their brother, he also didn't hesitate to kiss a girl—or argue with her—in full view of a crowded bar. The idea of holding his relationship with Tess up for their speculation…

The familiar creak of the front door heralded his arrival. None of the three Calhoun men seated looked away from the sports highlights on the big-screen television.

"Your mama just took Little Bit upstairs to brush her teeth," his father informed him. "There's beer in the fridge if you want to stay for a few minutes. And leftovers, too. Erin made her famous chicken dumplings."

Nick crossed the dark kitchen and filled a glass with cold water. "I had dinner in town. That's why I needed y'all to babysit, remember?"

"Oh, right." Wyatt turned in his recliner. "Big date. How'd it go?"

Kevin snorted. "How do you *think?* He's here with us, isn't he? If it had gone halfway decent, he'd be doing the mattress mambo with— Who were you with?"

"None of your damn business," Nick said matter-of-factly.

Their father jabbed a finger at Kevin. "Watch your mouth. You know your mama doesn't like you talking about the union between man and woman with such disregard."

It warmed Nick's heart to see his towering brother blush like a ten-year-old who'd just been given his first detention. "I'm going upstairs to get Bailey." His parents had assured him she could spend the night here if need be. Since that was sadly not the case, he might as well take her home where she could sleep in her own bed.

Bay sat propped against the headboard of his parents' bed, dressed in a pair of glaringly mismatched pajamas—a pink top printed with neon cowboy boots and green pants, striped in yellow and blue. Amid the boots was a splotch that looked suspiciously like chocolate ice cream. "Daddy! Gramma was about to read me a story. You can listen with us."

His mother was less effusive about his presence. "We didn't expect you this early."

He laughed wryly. "Should I leave and come back?"

"Of course not. It isn't that I'm unhappy to see you. I guess I just hoped you'd take me up on my offer to let Bailey stay the night. In case you and your friend decided to… have a tea party," she improvised.

Nick spluttered, choking on his water. "A tea party?" he

wheezed. Was that what they were calling it these days? "Mother, it was a first date! And it wasn't exactly a date, anyway. Although there were dinner and dancing."

"What about a *k-i-s-s* good-night?" Erin prompted, her eyes twinkling.

"*Mom.* Honestly, you're worse than Kevin."

"Don't be absurd, dear. No one is worse than Kevin. Between his inability to go out with a nice girl twice in a row and Wyatt's holding pattern with that rodeo woman, you may be my only shot at grandchildren. Poor Bailey wants brothers and sisters. She told me."

Nick rolled his eyes. "Now it's siblings, too? Last I heard, the wish list stopped with being a flower girl and having a new mommy come live with us."

"I thought Miss Tess was gonna help you find someone to be my mommy," Bailey piped up. "But I still think it should be her! She said you were tractor...um, tractive?"

"Attractive," Nick said. Definitely time to change the subject. "So what did you do this evening, kiddo?"

She beamed. "Grandad and I saw a poisonous snake out by the pond and Uncle Wyatt said maybe next time he helps babysit, he'll teach me to shoot a rifle."

"Like hel—" At the piercing look from his mother, Nick quickly amended his word choice. "Heck. You're not old enough for that."

Venomous snakes and guns? Bailey definitely needed more feminine influence in her life. It was becoming easier and easier to adjust to the idea of someday remarrying. Perhaps because he'd met someone he could see himself falling in love with.

"This is awful." Tess lay sprawled across the sofa in the main room of the B and B, an arm thrown over her eyes. Although there were two couples checked in to the establishment, they were currently on a trail ride with Sam. Tess and Lorelei had the place to themselves, leaving Tess free to vent about her wanton behavior the previous night. "Can you believe I made out with him?"

"I'm not seeing the problem." Lorelei sat in a nearby chair, feet tucked beneath her while Oberon the cat stalked in circles around her, still deciding whether he would deign to let her cuddle him. "You kissed the hot cowboy. Yippee, I say. Did I mention you're entitled to a 'plus one' at the wedding?"

Tess glared from beneath her arm. "Many times." She sat suddenly, swinging her legs to the floor. "You're forgetting his long-running interest in Farrah Landon."

"Yet he wasn't kissing *her.*"

"Well, no. She wasn't the one convenient. She wasn't the one standing in front of him, undressing him with her eyes. If she had been…" Would he have kissed Farrah with the same passion he'd shown Tess? Would he have bothered to stop if it had been Farrah in his arms, or would the two of them have made love through the night—the way Tess had dreamed of once she'd finally fallen into a fitful sleep?

Tess sighed. "I think I'll take you up on that offer of coffee if it still stands."

When she'd first arrived at the B and B, Lorelei had volunteered to get her a beverage and a breakfast pastry; Tess had felt too miserable to enjoy either. Instead, she'd flung herself onto the couch and into her recriminations. But given her lack of rest, if she didn't get some caffeine in her system soon, she could become a hazard to herself and others.

The two women went to the kitchen, Oberon following them in case there were treats to be had.

Lorelei poured two steaming mugs. "Okay, Nick liked Farrah at some point. They were never a couple, though. He is allowed to change his mind and develop feelings for someone else." She leaned across the counter and lightly bopped Tess on the head. "This means you."

"Over her already? He seems…steadier than that. He's not his brother, chasing after a different woman every week. He can commit. Nick's the only one among them who's been married." *And speaking of his marriage…* The confession he'd made about his feelings for Marla plagued her.

"I know he wouldn't appreciate my talking about him," Tess began, dumping sugar in her coffee. "But you're one of my best friends and if I can't discuss—"

"My lips are sealed. Tell me anything you want, and it'll go no further," Lorelei promised.

"You mean like when you told Heather I was trying to fix him up with Farrah?"

Lorelei winced. "Okay, that was unfortunate. But I really thought she knew. From here on out, no more mistakes like that."

"He confided to me that one of the reasons he proposed to his ex was because he was so comfortable with her."

"Makes sense. You certainly wouldn't want to marry someone who makes you *un*comfortable on a daily basis."

"Yeah, but… When Sam walks into a room, there's that zing between the two of you. Your first thought is *not* that he's as comfortable as a broken-in pair of sneakers. To some degree, Nick found her safe and convenient. What if he's ducking his feelings for Farrah because they aren't so safe?" Taking the easy way out, as it were.

"And what about you?" Lorelei reproached softly. "Did you come here hoping I'd talk you out of a discomfiting emotional risk? No one gets it more than me, how unpleasant it can be to make yourself vulnerable. But trust me, the rewards of loving and letting yourself be loved back…" She trailed off, fiddling with her engagement ring. Her expres-

sion as she contemplated life with Sam was more eloquent
than any words she could have used.

Tess stared through the kitchen window at the picturesque
flower garden, not wanting to face her slim, accomplished,
genius-with-numbers friend as she made this admission.
"You know what an understudy is, right? The alternate who
learns all the steps for those times the show must go on but
the *real* star isn't able to take the stage? I've felt like that so
many times, Lor. The perennial bridesmaid, the younger sister who never fully earned her parents' respect, the dancer
who was good enough for corps but never solos. I'm waiting
for my chance to shine, to star in my own life. I've never let
my pride make decisions for me, but I can't budge on this
one principle. I can't be anyone's backup plan."

Tess wasn't a kid anymore, content to go to prom with
her crush because his first choice couldn't make it. She'd
rather never see Nick again than see more of him because
he found her easier to talk to and less intimidating than the
woman he *really* wanted.

Chapter Nine

Standing behind the microphone at the front of the school cafeteria, the PTA president clasped her hands in front of her ample boson. "Why, Mr. Calhoun! Thank you for your willingness to help. I thought it would take more wheedling on my part to talk someone into chairing the committee."

Committee? What? He looked around the room at some of the other parents' expressions. Amusement and pity were the chief responses; one single mother whose twins had once celebrated their birthday at the Galloping C mimed a phone with her fingers. *Call me.*

Okay, so, going forward, he now knew to be very careful about standing up at PTA meetings. But the reason he'd bolted to his feet was because he'd spotted Heather Winchester in the hallway, speaking with the music teacher. He knew Heather had helped with costuming the children for the performance that would start once the PTA meeting ended.

He wanted to speak with Heather because she was close friends with Tess Fitzpatrick—the same Tess Fitzpatrick who seemed to be avoiding him. When she'd ushered him out of her house Saturday night, she'd told him to call her later. *Ha!* It was now Tuesday, and she'd yet to return any of his three messages.

Trying to cause as little disturbance as possible, he sidled to the edge of the cafeteria, then quickly exited the room.

"Mrs. Winchester?" He strode toward Heather.

Her friendly smile didn't mask the confusion in her gaze; they'd never spoken before and she was clearly surprised at being sought out. "What can I do for you?"

"Nick Calhoun." He shook her hand. "Our daughters are in the same dance class."

She nodded slowly. "Yes."

Now what? He'd been full of conviction when he'd hurried from his seat, but it wasn't as if he could demand to know why her friend had stopped speaking to him. He could understand that maybe he'd made a mistake in kissing Tess, but she wasn't a shrinking violet. He would have assumed she'd simply tell a guy he screwed up and move on from there. *He* was the one uncomfortable having conversations, not her.

Stalling as he tried to decide on a strategy, he said, "I understand your daughter Josie is one of the best in the class. Will she be doing a solo at next week's performance?"

At the mention of her daughter, Heather immediately softened, her quizzical expression replaced with maternal pride. "Yes, she is. She's so excited about it. She loves dance class."

"My girl's the same way. And no wonder—they have a great teacher, don't you think? I wanted to ask you about Tess. She specifically asked me to call her over the weekend, but she hasn't answered her phone. Have you seen her or talked to her? I'm starting to get a little worried."

Heather bit her lip, apparently unwilling to divulge whether she'd spoken to Tess. Was she afraid he'd press to know what her friend might have confided? "I'm sure she's fine. Probably spending extra time in the studio to get ready for the party next week."

"Probably. But would you do me a favor?" He flashed her the most charming smile he could muster. "If you see her, remind her to call me? Or, I guess I could just stop by the studio to check on her…" He trailed off, pleased with his stroke of ingenuity.

Judging by the way Heather's eyes had widened, she would no doubt pass along his words. He suspected he would hear from Tess very soon.

"I THOUGHT THIS GUY HAD difficulty talking to women?" Heather said disbelievingly.

"What guy?" Lean, rugged Zane Winchester strolled into his kitchen, his cowboy hat in hand. His voice was a playful mock growl as he put his arm around his wife's waist. "Should I be jealous?" After he'd kissed her cheek, he turned to smile at Tess, who was rinsing lettuce at the sink. "Hey, Tess, staying for dinner?"

Heather nodded. "I insisted."

Truthfully, Tess was grateful not to be at home. As long as she was busy, she had a legitimate excuse for not calling Nick yet. She did plan to call him, truly—she just hadn't figured out what to say. Also, she rationalized that by not being available, she was taking away his crutch. Maybe he'd work up the gumption to call Farrah instead.

"Well, we're glad to have you." Zane snagged a piece of the cucumber his wife had just sliced for the salad. "I know the girls will be thrilled. Josie worships you and ever since you helped Eden with her hair and makeup for the homecoming dance, she definitely thinks you're cooler than me."

Heather laughed. "She's sixteen, and you're her dad. She thinks pretty much the entire world is cooler than you."

He narrowed his eyes. "Watch it. You're still under suspicion because you haven't told me who this mysterious 'guy' is and I know all the places you're most ticklish." He glanced around as if suddenly realizing how quiet the house was. "Where are the girls?"

"Josie spent the afternoon at the Hollingers' playing with

their daughter. Eden just walked over to bring her home for supper. Go wash up. We'll be ready to eat in about fifteen minutes."

Zane grinned. "Is 'go wash up' code for 'get the heck out of the kitchen so Tess and I can talk privately'?"

"You Rangers don't miss a clue, do you? Now, shoo."

"I'm going, I'm going."

Not for the first time, Tess thought how perfect the Winchesters were together. The fact that they'd overcome secrets and difficult odds to find happiness was uplifting. *I will find the right man for me. Eventually.* And when she did, he wouldn't be smitten with someone else.

Heather swept all the chopped vegetables from the cutting board into the salad bowl. "I thought he'd never leave! We've only got a few minutes before the girls get back, so we have to talk fast. Josie's got radar ears, so it's impossible to have a private conversation with her in the house, and if Eden catches on that we're talking about a boy, she'll want in on the conversation, too."

Tess thought of the intense way Nick had kissed her Saturday. "I don't think 'boy' applies." He was all man. She picked up the conversation from where Zane had interrupted. "So explain to me what happened at this PTA meeting?"

"He cornered me in the hall to ask about you. He was charming and determined, not a shy bone in his body." Heather gave her a teasing smile. "I think you cured him. But I don't understand why you haven't called him. What gives, Fitzpatrick? When I was fighting my feelings for Zane early on, you were constantly nagging me to go ring his doorbell and make a move, lay it all on the line."

"This is different."

Heather put her hands on her hips, her expression the same one she used whenever Josie sneaked cookies she wasn't supposed to have or petted a strange dog without first asking an adult's permission. "How?"

"Because...it's *my* heart on the line," Tess said weakly. Oh, hell. She sounded pitiful even to herself. "I'll call him. Tonight after dinner, I promise. Unless I'm here late. That would be rude. He works such long hours at the ranch, and I wouldn't want to wake Bai—"

"You'll be leaving early."

"And to think I believed you were a friend," Tess groused, crossing the kitchen to pull salad dressing out of the refrigerator.

Heather laughed. "As *someone* I know frequently says, people often need a nudge in the right direction. Consider yourself officially nudged."

"Got any pointers on what to say to him?"

"Just be honest. If I've learned anything over the last year, it's the importance of telling the truth, no matter how bad it is." Her tone turned sympathetic. "And, unless I'm way off base, I'd say you've got it pretty bad."

Tess sighed. "I even like it when he calls me Contessa."

"But you hate your full name!"

"Not the way Nick says it." She didn't hate anything about Nick—except how insecure he suddenly made her feel.

From the moment she'd kissed him, she hadn't been behaving like herself. It was time to talk, to tell him he'd officially graduated Romance 101 and send him on his way. Then she'd be free to start getting over him.

WHEN NICK SAW TESS'S NUMBER on his cell phone, he wanted to pump his fist in victory. "It was the threat of my tracking you down in person, wasn't it?" he gloated.

"Polite people say 'hello,'" she retorted, sounding miffed. "I might even accept 'hey' or, under limited circumstances, 'whazzzzup?'"

He reached for the remote and muted his television. Tess got his full attention. "You've been avoiding me."

"Very true." Instead of denying it, she simply owned it. That was his Tess.

"Why?" Hadn't she missed him at all? He'd been going nuts thinking about her.

"I needed to think—"

"Because I kissed you? Should I apologize for that?"

Her breath hitched, a soft, vulnerable sound. "I needed to think about Operation Cupid."

"That's over." He hadn't thought about Farrah in days. He could not care less who she went with to the town's Valentine dance.

"I agree. I think you're ready—you don't need me anymore."

"I do! Not for asking out Farrah—I don't even want to do that. But because…" *Damn it.* Now was not the time to get tongue-tied!

"You should ask her to coffee, at the very least, to prove to yourself that you can. Spend a few hours with her, see if there are sparks. You owe it to yourself to find out." The false cheer in her voice faded as she added softly, "No woman wants to be second choice."

His free hand tightened into a fist. What could he say? Words bounced around his skull, useless in their disjointed state. In a warped way, she was right. It had taken him longer to notice her, to *know* her. But now that he had… What would soothe her without sounding like manipulative flattery? What would convince her of his feelings without scaring her off? He still didn't know if she felt the same way.

"Goodbye, Nick."

Apparently not.

AT THE END OF FRIDAY'S dance class, Tess's gaze caught on her own reflection in the mirror that ran the length of the studio wall. *Jeez. I look like hell.* No doubt caused by her lack of sleep lately. On the upside, she was also experiencing a marked lack of appetite, so maybe she really would lose five pounds before Lorelei's wedding. There you go, a silver lining.

She forced a smile for the girls. "That's it for today. I'll see you all next week for our special Valentine's Day performance!" She doled out hugs, squeezing Bailey with extra affection.

"When are you coming over for ninja tea party?" the little girl asked.

"Um…" *When I start dating some hunky fireman who heals my heart and makes it possible for me to be in the same room with your daddy without aching.* "Not sure."

If the universe was kind, Nick wouldn't be the one to pick up Bailey after class. Some evenings, it was Erin who came to get her granddaughter. Tess was glad when Mrs. Showalter asked for a registration form for the special dance camp Tess would be holding during spring break. It gave Tess a reason to go into the little storage room where the file cabinet sat. Whoever was picking up Bailey could come and go without Tess even noticing at all.

"Contessa?"

She resisted the urge to bang her head repeatedly on the cabinet. "You know, there are stalking laws…" She turned, freezing when she came face-to-face with a dozen red roses. "What are those?"

"Flowers," Nick said. "For you."

"Have you lost your mind?" Aware that her studio was full of parents who wouldn't want their daughters taught by a shrieking psychopath, she lowered her voice to an angry hiss. "I told you I wasn't interested! And you know darn well that Bailey is already emotionally attached to me. This isn't fair to her. Did she see those? She'll misunderstand."

"Or she'll understand perfectly. I want to be with you, Tess."

She squeezed her eyes shut, unprepared to deal with this full-court press. Why was it that hearing something part of her so desperately wanted made her want to cry? "You've obviously forgotten what I'm looking for in a guy. I need to be with someone who *listens,* remember? Someone who takes what I'm saying seriously?"

"You also want to be with someone who thinks you're 'worth the trouble of pursuing.'" He gave her a wolfish grin. "See? I listen."

NICK SAT THROUGH DINNER at The Twisted Jalapeño distracted, only half hearing his brother lean out of his side of the booth to flirt with owner Grace Torres when she walked by.

"When are you going to realize you're crazy about me," Kevin drawled, "and leave that pretty-boy chef?"

The beautiful brunette shot him a look so disdainful it could wither crops. "I think the phrase you were looking for is 'Greek god.' And, FYI, not only does my husband have a possessive streak, I'm pretty sure he could come up with twenty different ways to poison you and make it look like an accident." Then she gave the four of them the gracious smile she was known for. "Y'all enjoy your meal now."

Tim laughed out loud while Kevin eyed his burrito plate suspiciously.

"Miss Grace wouldn't really let her husband poison us, would she?" Bailey asked, sounding more excited than alarmed by the idea.

"Definitely not," Nick said. "Miss Grace worked too hard to keep this restaurant open to risk it being investigated by the police or closed by the Health Department. So, no worries. Eat up."

"Eat what? I'm all done," Bailey said.

"Already?" To cover the fact that he hadn't been paying attention, he added, "That was fast."

From across the table, Kevin stared at him as if he were crazy. "We've been here forty-five minutes. How long do you think it should take her to eat a taco?"

"Daddy, can I be 'scused to say hi to my friend Ashlee?"

Two tables away, a little girl from Bailey's kindergarten class sat with her parents.

"Sure." Nick rose from the bench seat to allow her to pass. "Tell her folks I said hi. And ask her mom if she'd like to help on a PTA committee," he said as an afterthought. When he sat back down, he noticed that Tim and Kevin were both giving him speculative looks.

"What?" he asked defensively.

"You tell us," Tim said. "Your mind's been elsewhere since you and Bailey met us here after her dance class. But you were focused when we were working with that new horse this afternoon. What happened between now and then?"

Kevin smirked. "I'm betting he ran into a certain blonde."

No, a redhead, you know-it-all.

"That's right!" Tim snapped his fingers. "Doesn't Farrah have a little ballerina, too?"

"What the hell is everyone's preoccupation with Farrah Landon?"

Kevin and Tim exchanged glances. For a moment, neither spoke, then Kevin ventured, "I can't speak for 'everyone,' but I can tell you what stays on my mind. Her—"

"Oh, stop being an ass for ten seconds," Nick interrupted. "What are you going to do when you've annoyed all the females in a hundred-mile radius and none of them will date you?"

"Grow old alone," Tim said at the exact same time Kevin answered, "Relocate."

"It *is* a woman who's got you this riled," Tim clarified. "Right?"

"Yes. But it's not Farrah Landon. I barely remember what I liked about her."

"Well," Kevin began. "She's got—"

Nick brandished his fork menacingly. "Don't make me stab you." Vowing to ignore his brother, he looked back at Tim. "I think I liked the idea of Farrah. I had a crush on her as a teenager, and it resurfaced now that we're both divorced single parents. But I don't really *know* her, Farrah the adult. Tess, on the other hand—"

"Tess Fitzpatrick? The curvy redhead?" Kevin asked with interest. At Nick's glare, Kevin stood suddenly. "Service is a little slow tonight. Think I'll mosey over to the bar to get my beer refilled."

"Tess, huh?" Tim gave his boss an assessing look. "Good choice. I like her."

"Yeah. Me, too." Understatement of the year. The question now was, how did he get her to accept his feelings? To admit that she returned them? He didn't want to come on too strong—the world had Kevin for that—but he didn't want to give up easily on something his gut told him could be so perfect. Even Bailey saw how good he and Tess could be together and she was only six!

Staring into space as he pondered his next move, his gaze caught on Sam Travis and Lorelei Keller. There were two people who understood what it took to make a relationship work. Would they be willing to give him advice? He remembered that not so long ago, he wouldn't have wanted to discuss his emotions for a woman or admit that he could use a hand. But everything was different now. Tess had changed his outlook.

She'd changed him.

"Be right back, Tim." He walked over to Sam and Lorelei's table, surprised when Lorelei smiled brightly.

"Is it my turn?" she asked.

"What?" His step faltered.

"Well, you've already accosted Heather. I'm the next logical choice."

Sam's eyebrows rose. "You've been accosting married women?"

"He's trying to enlist allies," Lorelei said, seeming very cheerful about his predicament. "To woo Tess."

"Ah." Sam shook his head in sympathy. "Good luck. It's a joy to have a woman in your life, but they can be hell to figure out."

"Hey!" Lorelei objected, looking not at all annoyed.

Sam grinned at her. "Whatever hell you might've caused me, you were worth it, darlin'."

"I know your loyalties are to Tess," Nick said, "but I'm striking out here."

"What is it you want from me, to put in a good word? Because I've already done that," Lorelei assured him. "Personally, I think she's crazy about you."

The surge of pure joy was staggering. It was an unimaginable relief to hear the words, even if they weren't from Tess herself. "I'm crazy about her, too."

"So what's the problem?" Sam asked. "Why aren't you off somewhere with Tess telling *her* how you feel, instead of interrupting date night?"

"I've tried. She doesn't want to listen." His gaze narrowed on Lorelei. "Do you know why? Is it really the Farrah thing? My crush on her dates back to adolescence. I'm sure Tess had plenty of crushes, too."

Lorelei squirmed under the invisible weight of confidences she felt bound to keep. Loyalty and discretion were admirable traits, but, oh, what Nick wouldn't give right now for loose-lipped women eager to spill secrets.

When she finally spoke, her words were disappointingly unhelpful. "Do you have a perfect relationship with your older brothers?"

"If you think that's a valid question, you're obviously an only child."

"True. But Tess isn't. Maybe you should ask her sometime what it was like to grow up in the same house as her stunning, blonde, prima-ballerina sister. That's all I can give you without betraying a friend. You'll have to take it from there."

"Thanks." He wasn't sure yet how she'd helped him, but he appreciated the effort.

"You're welcome." She grinned. "Now get lost. It's date night."

Chapter Ten

It was the type of Friday night perfect for eating frozen yogurt straight out of the carton and watching a DVD she'd seen so many times she'd memorized all the lines. Wearing a dark green tank top with plaid flannel pajama bottoms, Tess crossed her kitchen, refusing to look at the vase of flowers on the counter. Why had she even brought them home?

She'd tried to avoid taking them from Nick at the studio, glad when Mrs. Showalter had impatiently poked her head into the storage room to ask if Tess had found those registration forms yet. Between Tess helping other parents and Bailey declaring that her stomach was making "funny hungry noises," Nick had gone peacefully. But he'd left the roses on her desk.

When was the last time a man had brought her flowers? It was difficult not to be moved by the gesture. *Maybe you should just go out with him.* Of course, if things didn't work out between them—if one day realized he'd settled for something comfortable and wanted more—his daughter would be crushed. *She's not the only one.*

Tess rubbed her forehead. Behind her eye, there was a stress knot so big she was considering naming it. But she'd cured many a bad mood before with help from *The Princess Bride.* Grabbing her fro-yo and a spoon, she headed to the living room where Westley and Buttercup awaited. The knock at the door just as she was passing startled her enough that the spoon hit the floor with a metallic clatter.

"I'm not home," she called, her voice unapologetically cranky.

"Open the door," Nick said. "It's me."

I know it's you. That's why I don't want to open the door! She swung it wide. "Look—"

"This isn't stalking. It's a final appeal. Hear me out, and if you want me to go, this will be the last time I darken your doorstep."

"You can come in," she said guardedly. "But I am not sharing the cookie-dough yogurt."

"Tough terms, but I accept."

As soon as he stepped inside, she had a memory of the last time he'd been here, so vivid it was almost physical. Her body burned at the mental replay of how he'd backed her against the wall and seduced her mouth with a kiss hotter than—

"Tess." His voice had gone hoarse, and his eyes sparked with desire. "This is ridiculous. If we both want each other so badly—"

"You're calling me ridiculous? Not a good start, Romeo."

She retreated into the living room, partly to put down the cold carton in her hand but more to put distance between them. Nick rarely asked out a woman. And when he did, by his own admission, he half hoped they'd say no. So what did it say about him that he was here now, after she'd already pushed him away?

Rather than come any closer, he sat on the edge of her couch. She paced, too edgy to get comfortable in a chair.

"It wasn't my brothers' fault that I had a speech impediment," he said out of the blue. "But they certainly didn't make it any easier. They picked on me until Dad threatened to tan their hides, but even if they hadn't been openly mocking, it still would have been difficult. Everything always came so damn easily to them. Junior-rodeo trophies, girlfriends, 4-H ribbons, touchdowns on the football team. Was that how it was with your sister?"

"Regina didn't play football."

"I'm opening up to you over here. Can't you meet me halfway?"

Her fingers curled into fists at her sides. "What do you want me to say, that it sucks being the ugly duckling when your sister's the boyfriend-stealing swan? Not that he was actually my boyfriend and, technically, he liked her first…"

Thick anger clogged Nick's mind—not anger at her, but for her. How could she ever have seen herself as "ugly" anything? How could her family have allowed that? And how was he going to trump an insecurity that had been building throughout her life?

"You've been lying, Tess, to me and to yourself. You act like, if I don't go out with Farrah, I'll always wonder what would have happened. But *you're* the one who would wonder. How can you worry that I'd rather be with her when I'm right here, telling you I want to be with you?"

"Nick, you said yourself that when you proposed to your wife, you thought it was the right thing to do at the time. Is that how you feel about it now?"

"She gave me Bailey." He would always be grateful for that. "I don't regret my marriage."

"Will you regret cowardice?" she flung at him. "Settling for someone instead of taking a chance with your 'dream girl'?"

"When I was fourteen! Her cheerleading uniform was probably a strong factor. But I'm not fourteen anymore."

"Neither am I," she said stubbornly. "When I was younger, I would have gone along with a guy who'd seen me as a buddy, who was comfortable and had fun with me, and thought that was enough for a relationship. I deserve more."

His jaw clenched. "People think I'm the one who lacks confidence, but *you're* the one about to throw away the chance at something truly special. I thought you were braver."

A small sob caught in her throat. "Which just proves what I've been saying, Nick. You're wrong about me."

ALTHOUGH SHE HAD A STANDING invitation to join her parents for supper on Sunday evenings, Tess usually declined. She wasn't sure whether her showing up now stemmed from the need to be around people after a miserable Saturday night alone reliving Nick's words, or if joining her parents was some sort of self-imposed penance for hurting him. He'd mostly looked furious when he stormed out of her house the other night, but, beneath that, she'd glimpsed the wounded expression in his steely gaze.

That had haunted her. If she had the power to hurt him, then he obviously cared for her. The question was, how much?

It had been so tempting to give in to him, but she'd resisted. Shouldn't she be proud of the discipline it had taken to stand by her decision? The easy thing, the weaker thing, would have been to drag him into her bedroom and let herself pretend that he'd chosen her out of preference, rather than default.

"Contessa! There you are." Gillian Fitzpatrick leaned in to give her a quick peck on the cheek before ushering her into the pot-roast-scented house. "Why don't you give your father your coat to hang up? Howard, take the girl's coat!"

As Tess shrugged out of the jacket, she felt the prickle of her mother's critical gaze. *What now?* She didn't have to wait long to discover the source of Gillian's dissatisfaction.

"Do you ever use that flatiron I gave you at Christmas?"

"No, I returned it and got an electric ice-cream maker," Tess said defiantly.

Her mother gasped. "What has gotten into you? I didn't raise you to be rude."

Says the woman who usually starts pointing out my flaws within fifteen seconds of my walking through the door. Since Tess couldn't quite bring herself to apologize sincerely, she simply said, "I didn't sleep well last night." *Or the past six consecutive nights.* "I may not be fit company." Was it too late to turn around and go home?

Gillian pressed her lips into a thin line. "Let's just focus on what's important—family. At least I have one of my daughters here. Lord knows when your sister will be able to visit again! Regina is dancing *Giselle* to sold-out houses and as soon as that wraps, she'll have to start rehearsals on *Romeo and Juliet.*"

"Well, I'm glad you have me as a backup between her visits," Tess said.

Her mother either missed or chose to overlook the sarcasm. "We should eat before the roast gets cold. Why hasn't your father come back? It doesn't take that long to hang up a coat. Howard!"

Tess followed her mother to the back of the house. Growing up, the hallway had been decorated with family photos—the Fitzpatricks' wedding portrait, the girls' school pictures. But Gillian Fitzpatrick had redecorated to spotlight a common theme. Silver frames contained large black-and-white prints of Regina; most of them were ballet shots but there were also several of her in her wedding dress. In none of them did her hair have the bad manners to frizz or curl. Tess had sometimes wondered where the other pictures had gone, but she never asked. She wasn't sure she was ready to hear that her high-school graduation photo now lived in the attic.

The food smelled divine, but by the time they reached the kitchen, Tess had no appetite left. Why, on a day when she needed comfort, had she chosen to come here? *Must have confused my family with someone else's.*

Gillian's heels clicked sharply across the Spanish tile as she carried dishes to the table. "Your father's sulky because I didn't make dessert, but I knew you'd appreciate my restraint. How's the weight loss going for your friend's wedding?"

"Swell. In fact, don't be surprised if I barely eat anything," Tess said.

Her father said the blessing. No sooner had they all said, "Amen" than Gillian said, "When you called to tell me you were coming for dinner, I half expected you to bring a guest."

"You did? Why?" Tess had never once subjected anyone else to one of these strained meals.

"Bitsy Harper said she saw you out last weekend on a date. She seemed to think it looked…" Gillian shot a glance toward her husband before dropping her voice. "Passionate. I do hope you were comporting yourself with decorum?"

"Oh, for crying out… I danced with him. Once. That was all." But, Lord, what a dance. Tess stabbed at her mashed potatoes. She wished she were somewhere with Nick now. "Bitsy Harper has an overactive imagination. Nick and I—"

"Nicholas Pfeffer?" her mother asked, her eyes gleaming. "The lawyer?"

"No, Nick Calhoun. The cowboy," Tess added with relish.

Gillian frowned. "The one who stutters?"

Right, because heaven forbid one of Gillian's daughters date someone with a defect. Would it do any good if Tess pointed out that he hadn't stuttered in *years* but that even if he did, he was a kind, loyal, sexy man with an adorable daughter and a gift with horses? "Yes, the one who stuttered. But it could be worse, right? He could have *frizzy hair!*"

"Why are you raising your voice to me?" Gillian looked genuinely shocked. "Howard, tell her not to raise her voice at the table."

Tess stood. "I shouldn't have come." Not when she was apparently spoiling for a fight. She'd spent her teenage years arguing with her mother and it had accomplished nothing. What was the point in wasting her breath now and ruining her parents' dinner?

"Contessa Gretchen Fitzpatrick, you sit down and finish your meal." Her mother pointed at the chair. "Honestly. You know, your sister would never behave like this."

"Trust me, I am aware. If I knew how to be more like Regina, Mom... Don't you think I would have loved the solos, the boyfriends, the approval from my parents?" Tears blurred her vision, and Tess hurried to the kitchen, wanting to be alone when they finally fell.

She leaned over the counter, pressing her hands to her eyes in a futile attempt to stem the flow. The *click, click* of Gillian's heels wrung a damp groan from her.

"Not now, Mom."

"Shush. Mothers know best." Her mom stood beside her and, for a brief second, put her arm around Tess's shoulders and squeezed. It wasn't much as hugs went, but Gillian had never been demonstratively affectionate. "Now, what's this really about?"

Because a lifetime of resentment at being a second-class citizen in her own family wasn't enough of a reason to snap?

"You've always been outspoken, but you're not typically this emotional," Gillian said. "So what's changed? Is it this Nick?"

Yes. "Despite whatever Bitsy told you, he and I are not a couple. I am single." Utterly and spectacularly single.

"Well, you've always been a very independent person. Not everyone is meant to be in a relationship."

"Jeez, Mom! You don't have to make it sound as if I'll die alone. I *want* to be in a relationship. Regina's not the only one who's dreamed of a big white wedding and her day in the sun as a beautiful bride. I deserve happiness, too." Her voice broke. "Don't I?"

"Tessie."

Both women turned in surprise to find Howard Fitzpatrick standing in the doorway of the kitchen. He locked gazes with his daughter, his eyes full of compassion, and simply opened his arms. Tess threw herself into the bear hug, letting her father soothe her as if she were a little girl. She sniffed, trying not to cry all over his polo shirt.

He held her silently, proving what she'd told Nick once. Sometimes, the words didn't matter. It was okay if you didn't know what to say. Actions were more important anyway.

Hypocrite. If actions were so important, why was she clinging to Nick's words, hiding behind them as if they were a shield? Yes, he'd said his feelings for Farrah dated back years. Yes, he'd made it sound as if he'd once considered her the Holy Grail of girlfriends. But those were statements, not actions.

His dance with Tess—that had been an action. Kissing her. Coming to her house the other night. Bringing her flowers.

Was she letting her own insecurities and a few words stand in the way of the happiness she claimed to deserve?

IT WAS STRANGE FOR NICK to enter the high school Monday evening. He himself had graduated from this school, but that seemed like an alternate universe. There was a disconnect between the kid he'd been and the man escorting his nervous daughter to the auditorium. Her hair was tamed into a sleek dark bun and she wore a red leotard with white tights. He was supposed to deliver her backstage so she could get her tutu and some light makeup. Tess was using this as a way to prepare some of the younger dancers for the much-more-complicated spring recital.

Nick had to admit, he wasn't particularly in a Valentine's mood, but he looked forward to watching his daughter dance. "You are going to be great!"

"My tummy feels funny," she admitted.

His, too. This would be the first time he'd seen Tess since his ill-advised plan of showing up at her house.

If the backstage area was a piece of artwork, it would have been titled "Pandemonium in Pink." Girls were giggling and crying and looking for a missing ballet slipper. Mothers were lacing tutus and applying makeup to little faces. Younger siblings were zipping around, ducking between the curtain panels despite repeated reminders that there was no running.

"Miss Tess!" Without waiting for Nick, Bailey ran up to the woman in the center of the chaos, hugging her beloved ballet teacher.

Nick actually experienced a moment's envy that she was allowed to express her affection so unreservedly. He settled for a crisp nod. "Miss Fitzpatrick."

Her gaze was surprisingly warm, like melting chocolate. "Actually, I prefer Contessa."

It wasn't so much her words that threw him as the timbre of her voice. Something had changed, but this probably wasn't the time or place to ask her what.

She swallowed. "Nick, I—"

"Tess, I can't get the music to work!" A teenager with a frantic expression and pink streaks in her blond hair approached Tess. "And Mom asked if we've got any more of those sequined bows?"

"Okay, be right there." Tess looked at Nick. "Can we talk after the performance? Please?"

He wasn't sure what she wanted to say, but he instinctively recognized the vulnerability in her voice. It echoed how he'd felt for the past week. Was there still a chance that she would believe what he'd been trying to tell her? "Absolutely. Anything I can do to help in the meantime?"

"Would you be willing to handle the door-prize announcements and take over raffle tickets? Heather was selling them, but we need her for last-minute costume emergencies. Unless you're handy with a needle and thread?" Tess's dimple appeared unexpectedly, and he badly wanted to kiss her.

"Raffle tickets it is."

A few minutes later, Heather had handed him the roll of tickets and the zipped pouch of cash. "Make sure people know it's for a good cause," she said. For each class at the dance studio, Tess held slots for a couple of students from lower-income families, girls who showed promise and a real love of dance but whose parents couldn't quite afford lessons. The raffle was to help with a fund that allowed those students to buy shoes and costumes.

Determined to make Tess proud and raise money for something important to her, he approached everyone—mothers, fathers, grandparents—and poured on as much charm as he could.

"I'll take ten," a female cooed.

When he turned, he saw Farrah smiling up at him. "That's great. It's for a worthy cause."

She laid a hand on his arm. "You are *such* a good father, getting involved like this. My ex probably won't even bother to show up and support his daughters, yet here you are. Volunteering backstage, getting involved at PTA meetings… I'm a little hurt, you know."

He blinked, having no idea what she was talking about. "You are?"

"I thought maybe you'd ask me to help with your committee." She flipped her blond hair over her shoulder. "I guess since you never asked me, I'll have to take matters into my own hands. Let me give you my number. I've chaired lots of committees. I could give you some pointers. Maybe over dinner?"

"That's nice, Farrah, but—" Looking past her, he spotted Tess. Even from this distance, the naked doubt was clear on her face. Just as he was sure that, from where she stood, Farrah's body language was clear. He doubted people on packed subways stood as close as Farrah was to him. He shuffled back a step. "I appreciate the offer, but my committee's pretty well staffed. I think they need some help with the science fair, though."

AS THE LAST STRAINS OF MUSIC faded softly, thunderous applause filled the high-school auditorium. Tess was so proud. Her girls had all done such a wonderful job today. And, frankly, she was proud of herself, too. Earlier, when she'd glanced across the room and seen Farrah blatantly hitting on Nick... It would have been easy to panic, to tell herself they made a stunning couple, that he should have a chance with Farrah to see if they were well suited.

She'd felt that way for exactly ten seconds. Then she'd realized, *Hell with that. He's mine.* Other women had had their chances. If they hadn't been able to see all the qualities Tess had always known Nick possessed, they didn't deserve him. She couldn't wait to dismiss everyone to the cafeteria, where Eden and some of her friends had set up refreshments, so that she could finally talk to Nick alone. But first, there was one last thing to take care of.

She stepped up to the microphone. "Thank you all so much for coming this evening. I know it means a lot to the girls. I also want to thank you for your support of the studio, which comes in many forms. Volunteer hours, bringing your daughters to extra rehearsals the month of recital, and even the simple act of buying raffle tickets so that we can give the gift of dance to even more girls in our community. I know many of you have bought tickets today and are waiting anxiously to find out if you're a winner. So, without any further ado, I'll turn this over to Nick Calhoun."

He came up the side steps of the stage, and Tess tried not to stare. How was it possible that she'd missed him so much in such a short period of time? She backed farther into the shadows, hoping the parents in the audience couldn't read her hungry expression when she looked at him. Nick stood a few feet in front of her, calling out the names of the winners. Tess realized that in addition to being proud of her students and herself, she was darn proud of him, too. It was difficult to believe that the man making jokes and reading off names was the same boy who'd stammered through childhood, speaking as little as possible and trying not to draw attention to himself.

The total opposite of me. She'd craved the spotlight since she was born. It was funny, how alike they truly were for all their seeming differences. Lost in her thoughts, she wasn't completely paying attention to Nick's words as he concluded.

"How about one last round of applause for the woman who made this all possible, Tess Fitzpatrick, the woman I love."

What? Her heartbeat rocketed. Without making a conscious decision to move, she bolted to his side, keeping her voice to a whisper. "What did you just say?"

He didn't bother lowering his own voice. "That I love you."

There were murmurs and a few chuckles in the audience. Tess heard a couple of *awww*s. She suspected Heather was among them.

Tess cupped her hand over the microphone, ignoring the screeched blare of feedback. "I…" She couldn't believe he thought this was an appropriate venue to share his feelings, but she was too ecstatic over what he'd said to object.

"Kiss him!" That was *definitely* Heather.

Nick's eyes twinkled. "I'm in favor of that suggestion."

"There are children in the room," Tess pointed out breath-lessly.

He gently lifted her hand from the microphone. "Folks, there are food and drinks in the cafeteria. Go enjoy them." Then he led Tess backstage.

"Why did you say that?" she whispered, stunned that this once reticent man had publicly proclaimed his feelings for her.

"Because it's true." Nick pulled her against him. "And I wanted you to know it, beyond a shadow of a doubt. No one else holds a candle to you. I may have called someone my dream girl, but that's what it was—a long-ago, insubstantial dream. What I feel for you is reality. In a lot of ways you woke me up. It's gotten easier to talk to people. I laugh more. Except for when you pushed me away. Don't do that again."

"Definitely not," she promised. She stretched up on her toes to kiss him, stopping at the very last second. "You really love me? Even after I nearly made a mess of this?"

"I love you." He brushed his thumb over her lower lip. It was amazing how such a slight touch could stoke such powerful desire. "And I never say anything I don't mean."

There was suddenly a flurry of motion—Bailey burst through the other side of the curtain, Heather hot on her heels.

"Sorry!" Heather exclaimed. "She got away from me."

Bailey launched herself in the middle of their embrace for a group hug. "Is Miss Tess going to be my new mommy?"

"Um…" Nick looked sheepish, as if only just realizing the consequences of his public declaration. "Let's not put Tess on the spot, kiddo. Maybe we should start with an easier question. Contessa, will you be my valentine?"

"*Our* valentine," Bailey said.

Tess smiled, so full of emotion it was difficult to speak. "Yes." Always.

* * * * *

COMING NEXT MONTH
from Harlequin® American Romance®
AVAILABLE MARCH 5, 2013

#1441 COWBOY FOR KEEPS
Mustang Valley
Cathy McDavid

Conner Durham can't believe his luck—Dallas Sorrenson is finally single and free to date. Then he learns she's pregnant...and the father is the man who stole Conner's job.

#1442 BETTING ON TEXAS
Amanda Renee

City girl Miranda Archer buys a ranch in Texas, hoping to start over. But she has apparently stolen it from Jesse Langtry—a cowboy who's rugged, gorgeous and madder than hell at her!

#1443 THE BABY JACKPOT
Safe Harbor Medical
Jacqueline Diamond

After an unexpected night with sexy surgeon Cole Rattigan, nurse Stacy Layne discovers she's pregnant. But her recent donation of eggs to a childless couple means her hormones have gone wild. Result: she's carrying triplets!

#1444 A NANNY FOR THE COWBOY
Fatherhood
Roxann Delaney

Luke Walker desperately needs a nanny for his young son. Hayley Brooks needs a job. It's a perfect match—in more ways than one!

HARCNM0213

REQUEST YOUR FREE BOOKS!

2 FREE NOVELS PLUS 2 FREE GIFTS!

HARLEQUIN

American ★ Romance®

LOVE, HOME & HAPPINESS

YES! Please send me 2 FREE Harlequin® American Romance® novels and my 2 FREE gifts (gifts are worth about $10). After receiving them, if I don't wish to receive any more books, I can return the shipping statement marked "cancel." If I don't cancel, I will receive 4 brand-new novels every month and be billed just $4.49 per book in the U.S. or $5.24 per book in Canada. That's a savings of at least 14% off the cover price! It's quite a bargain! Shipping and handling is just 50¢ per book in the U.S. and 75¢ per book in Canada.* I understand that accepting the 2 free books and gifts places me under no obligation to buy anything. I can always return a shipment and cancel at any time. Even if I never buy another book, the two free books and gifts are mine to keep forever.

154/354 HDN FVPK

Name	(PLEASE PRINT)
Address	Apt. #
City	State/Prov.	Zip/Postal Code

Signature (if under 18, a parent or guardian must sign)

Mail to the Harlequin® Reader Service:
IN U.S.A.: P.O. Box 1867, Buffalo, NY 14240-1867
IN CANADA: P.O. Box 609, Fort Erie, Ontario L2A 5X3

Want to try two free books from another line?
Call 1-800-873-8635 or visit www.ReaderService.com.

* Terms and prices subject to change without notice. Prices do not include applicable taxes. Sales tax applicable in N.Y. Canadian residents will be charged applicable taxes. Offer not valid in Quebec. This offer is limited to one order per household. Not valid for current subscribers to Harlequin American Romance books. All orders subject to credit approval. Credit or debit balances in a customer's account(s) may be offset by any other outstanding balance owed by or to the customer. Please allow 4 to 6 weeks for delivery. Offer available while quantities last.

Your Privacy—The Harlequin® Reader Service is committed to protecting your privacy. Our Privacy Policy is available online at www.ReaderService.com or upon request from the Harlequin Reader Service.

We make a portion of our mailing list available to reputable third parties that offer products we believe may interest you. If you prefer that we not exchange your name with third parties, or if you wish to clarify or modify your communication preferences, please visit us at www.ReaderService.com/consumerschoice or write to us at Harlequin Reader Service Preference Service, P.O. Box 9062, Buffalo, NY 14269. Include your complete name and address.

HARI3

Welcome back to MUSTANG VALLEY,
and Cathy McDavid's final book in this series.
Conner Durham has gone from flashy executive to simple
cowboy seemingly overnight. At least Dallas Sorrenson
has appeared back in his life—and she's
apparently single!

The laughter, light and musical, struck a too-familiar chord. His steps faltered, and then stopped altogether. It couldn't be her! He must be mistaken.

Conner's hands involuntarily clenched. Gavin wouldn't blindside him like this. He'd assured Conner weeks ago that Dallas Sorrenson had declined their request to work on the book about Prince due to a schedule conflict. Her wedding, Conner had assumed.

And, yet, there was no mistaking that laughter, which drifted again through the closed office door.

With an arm that suddenly weighed a hundred pounds, he grasped the knob, pushed the door open and entered the office.

Dallas turned immediately and greeted him with a huge smile. The kind of bright, sexy smile that had most men— Conner included—angling for the chance to get near her.

Except, she was married, or soon to be married. He couldn't remember the date.

And her husband, or husband-to-be, was Conner's former coworker and pal. The man whose life remained perfect while Conner's took a nosedive.

"It's so good to see you again!" Dallas came toward him.

He reached out his hand to shake hers. "Hey, Dallas."

With an easy grace, she ignored his hand and wound her arms loosely around his neck for a friendly hug. Against his better judgment, Conner folded her in his embrace and drew her close. She smelled like spring flowers and felt like every man's fantasy. Then again, she always had.

"How have you been?"

Rather than state the obvious, that he was still looking for a job and just managing to survive, he answered, "Fine. How 'bout yourself?"

"Great."

She looked as happy as she sounded. Married life obviously agreed with her. "And how is Richard?"

"Actually, I wouldn't know." An indefinable emotion flickered in her eyes. "As of two months ago, we're no longer engaged."

It took several seconds for her words to register; longer for their implication to sink in.

Dallas Sorrenson was not just single, she was available.

Look for COWBOY FOR KEEPS, coming this March 2013 only from Harlequin American Romance!